THROWN IN THE DEEP END

By the same author

GROWING TOWARDS THE LIGHT
GIRL WITH BLACK BAGS
THE DIVINE SPRINGTIME

For Chris and Joel with love

While based on true experiences, some names and
places are fictional

THROWN IN THE DEEP END

Stories of a travelled life

JULIET GRAINGER

CONTENTS

Orphanage Old Delhi

THROWN IN THE DEEP END

Ever since reading Malcolm Muggeridge's book 'Something Beautiful for God', I had wanted to go to India to help in the Mother Teresa Centres. Now here I was in a plane circling Calcutta, looking down at what looked like a green oasis, with lots of palm trees all around the airport. As I stepped out of the aeroplane the heat embraced me. It was incredibly hot. About 45 degrees centigrade.

The drive from the airport to Calcutta was along small roads, crowded with ancient cars, lorries, water buffalo cows, and people mingling with the traffic. A vulture landed on a tree ready for a picking of some bloated dead carcass, and this sight shocked me into realising that I had really arrived in India.

Calcutta is a very crowded city, and it is quite overwhelming when you first arrive. It just teems with a mass of thronging people, cars, bicycles, lorries and even the occasional camel and elephant. The taxi driving is hair-raising because, although officially they drive on the left in India, in reality they weave all over the road, around potholes and any obstacles in the way. It's always the largest vehicle or the one with the loudest horn that wins the right of way.

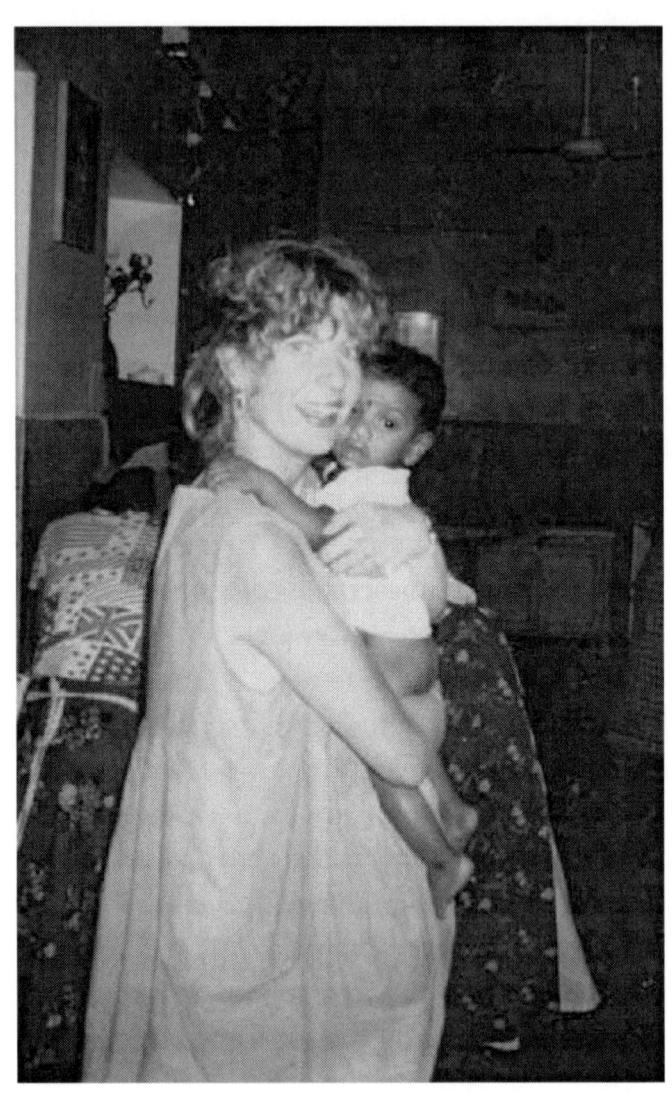

Crossing the road in India is similar. I felt I was taking my life in my hands every time I ventured out, as the drivers kept coming at me with their hands on their horns. After a couple of weeks an Indian friend taught me not to look at the oncoming cars, but instead to walk as if I hadn't noticed they were about to mow me down. This really seemed to help! The driver's game was lessened when they didn't see my terrified eyes begging them to avoid me!

I had expected to see poverty and to find the heat and humidity a strain, but nothing had prepared me for the onslaught of noise, or for the overpowering stench of stagnant festering rubbish and sewage. The first time I walked through the back streets, I thought I'd be sick, it was so overpowering.

The first Mother Teresa Centre I visited was 'Kaligat', the place for those picked up from the streets that were dying or critically ill. Kaligat is part of a Hindu temple. The temple is a very active place thronging with worshippers, children playing, scattered flowers, white cows, and sacrificial animals. It bustles all day with funerals and worship, and it is noisy like a market place.

After that the hush and tranquillity inside Kaligat was a real contrast As I walked through the main doorway I saw a notice in English saying 'The Mother Teresa Centre, no photos.'

The first room I passed through was the men's side. As my eyes became accustomed to the gloom, after the blazing hot sunshine outside, I saw the bodies of men, emaciated and huge eyed, lying on tiered pallets, some higher, some lower, a few sitting or crouching, but the majority lying. After the roar of the outside, the silence and peace of the place was all-enveloping.

I worked in the women's section, as female volunteers worked with the women, and male volunteers with the men. I was given an apron and then it was up to me to watch and see the routine, and to make myself useful. We - myself and volunteers from all over the world - started at eight in the morning and worked until midday. We would carry the women to a stone shelf next to a trough, and, with a tiny piece of soap and cups of water, we would wash them. Meanwhile, others would be changing their pallets. This task consisted of scrubbing a plastic sheet with a bucket of water, putting on a clean sheet if there was one to be found, and then laying the person back on the mat.

Afterwards it was time for medicine. Each pallet was numbered, and the 'sisters' would hand out the medicine for each number. Mostly it was vitamins; and when available, pain killers. Water cups were shared by all. Then came the time for feeding. As many of the women were too weak to feed themselves, we were free to go and choose the ones we knew needed feeding. Some could still squat in Indian fashion on the ground, next to the pallets, and feed themselves, always with the right hand. Others we fed with our right hands as they lay on their sides. The favorite food was fish heads and rice.

Most of the women were skeletal: stick thin

with their pelvic bones jutting out. There were terrible sores, and sometimes you could see the bones through holes in their skin. Strangely I never witnessed any real distress. Although in great discomfort they were peaceful. Their eyes were bright, and their energy and life force was strong. I came to the conclusion that these people had amazingly resistant constitutions and spirits. Just to survive to adulthood on the streets was proof of their immunity and will to live.

After the feeding and cleaning up, we swept the floor, crouching down with a hand brush of tied twigs. We also washed the dishes using ash to scrub with, while squatting over the huge cooking pots. We rinsed the plates in buckets of water.

Then came the wound dressing. There were only the bare necessities. Dressings, tweezers, and bandages made up from torn sheets. After we had made them more comfortable and the chores were finished, we were free to love these women. We could choose those who we felt needed us most, and sit with them and comfort them.

The response of these people was heart-tugging. As we came to know them over the days, their black eyes would light up on our arrival, and they would hold out their stick like arms, calling out in their different dialects for us to come to them. When I touched and stroked them, to give comfort, they would uncover their wounds like small children with a bad finger, for me to place my hands over their sores. They would hold my hands on their foreheads or clasped over their hearts, or wherever it was most necessary; and as I sat with them, they would hold my eyes with theirs chattering in Bengali, telling me their whole life story. The language, apart from a few words, I couldn't understand, but the communication, the feeling and the eye-talk, was understood by both. These people were so simple and so open. They understood that I was loving them through my hands, eyes and heart, and there was always a feeling of meeting, and of great response.

It was May and June when I was there. Daily the weather grew hotter and hotter as it built up towards the monsoons. On some days you could actually see when certain women had decided it was time for them to die. They gave up eating, refused all medicine, and they would peacefully lie there with no resistance. They seemed to die very gently and quietly, and all of us working there felt that the love and peace that filled that building had reached them. Sometimes they would hold my hands over their hearts as they drifted away. Others would lay their heads in my lap. This I later discovered was their way of saying I was their mother and father, which I felt to be a tremendous honour.

There were always strong messages and I felt a tremendous respect for their needs. I often wondered what these proud and beautiful Indian people thought about having foreigners caring for them. It was such a new experience.

Outside in the back streets of Calcutta there seemed to be suspicion and slight hostility when we walked through the streets. But in the centres I never saw any sign of this, only welcome and warmth in their eyes. It was always an intensely moving and profound experience.

One of the Mother Teresa Sisters in London summed up these people for me when she said,

'In India people speak with the language of love.'

I personally, found some of the work in Kaligat very hard when I first arrived, being unused to the sights, heat and smells. There was nowhere to hide any of the realities in this place, and clearing and cleaning up often had to be done with the bare hands. There were no tissues, no paper, and no scented disinfectants. Sometimes there were even no rags left. I often thought of the words: 'My Kingdom for a rag.'

How glad I was with my supply of wet wipes, carried around with me wherever I went, along with my water bottle.

I think now I can understand Mother Teresa's teaching when she tells us that unless we love Christ in these people, we cannot be of use. The more you became exposed to the work, the more you could cope with each day. Whereas in the early days I would guiltily avoid some of the goriest sights. In time I found I could tackle anything. Since I am normally pretty squeamish I was proud of myself. One thing India teaches its travellers is to accept all manner of extraordinary experiences.

Whilst in Calcutta I was lucky enough to be taken outside to visit the leprosorium. This experience affected me deeply, and has perhaps been the key that has led me to working with those with Aids in the present.

The leper colony just outside Calcutta is no longer run by the Mother Teresa Sisters, as some of the people with leprosy had been too violent for these women.

Now it is run by Brother Andrew and six brothers. They, I learnt, had a similar vocation to that of Mother Teresa. The farm where they live is on the side of a railway line. Those with leprosy, under the guidance of the brothers, have built the whole place. It is spotlessly clean with dormitories and even some family accommodation. They have cultivated the land around growing vegetables and keeping pigs, chickens and goats. Which animals they care for depends on their religious beliefs.

As in the Mother Teresa Centres, the different religious beliefs are deeply respected and encouraged. There is no Christian evangelising, only faith in action. It is wonderful to see how Muslims, Hindus, Sikhs, Christians, Baha'is and other groups can live and worship side by side, respecting each other's religious customs.

The main industry in this particular community is weaving cloth and sandal making. Those stricken with leprosy weave nearly all the cloth for the sisters' Saris, the bed sheets and bandages. Those who no longer have fingers are helped by those who have hands. Those who are blind are guided by those with sight. Even the handicapped can still be teachers to the able-bodied.

There was a tremendous feeling of comradeship,

sharing and mutual support, and I really felt the love of those men running the enterprise. The brother who showed me round was able to speak fifteen different dialects. He had done a medical course and had building and carpentry skills. I couldn't help thinking how many talents he had tapped into within himself. He really was a fulfilled man.

These people with leprosy had been given a reason to live again; they had purpose in their lives. They were able to marry and have families, knowing their children would be treated and be free of this terrible devouring disease. The great problem with this illness in India is that the people think they are getting better and stop the treatment. This can be fatal. Those who have lost eyes, fingers and hands have done so because they hid the symptoms under rags until it was too late. Others have had their fingers or toes gnawed by rats as they lay in the streets. They lose all feeling in these limbs so they are unaware it is happening.

This colony is also a clinic. Every week several thousand people came to have their wounds dressed and to take the medicine that treats leprosy. Most of these people had been abandoned by their families and relatives. Some had been wealthy and all had found themselves beggars and cast-offs, so their loneliness and sense of rejection must have been enormous.

I also spent time in a leprosorium outside Delhi. Here the farm was smaller, but vegetables were grown and the inhabitants did the cooking. The men and women again slept in separate dormitories and I was

free to walk around. Here many were terminally
ill. Very often with the blind ones I used to put my
hands over their eyes or hold their faces, as some
of these people had hands devoid of feeling. They
would sometimes weep with the joy of the contact,
and would place my hands over their hearts and, as in
the home for dying in Calcutta, they used to unwrap
their stumps and place them in my lap. They shared
themselves completely, and this is what I can never
forget. I feel I will keep on seeing those eyes and
expressions for the rest of my life. It was a joyous
experience.

There was one man in particular dying of TB.
He was having great difficulty in breathing, with
that now familiar death rattle that signified that he
had little time left. I knelt by his bed and sat him
up, while rubbing his labouring back and chest.
Suddenly, looking up, I saw all the rest of the men in
that dormitory standing round the bed. They were in
prayer with their hands clasped over their hearts. This
is called 'nemesti,' the greeting from the heart. They
were all loving this brother, sending him their love and
speeding him on his journey and I found this intensely
moving.

The last memory that lingers from this colony
is the beaming face of an eight-year-old boy, as he sat
protectively by his mother's side. Both her legs had
been amputated from below the knee. He had chosen
to come and live with her, even though he was free of
leprosy. She had remarried in the leprosorium and life
was again fulfilling for her. It was the boy's love and

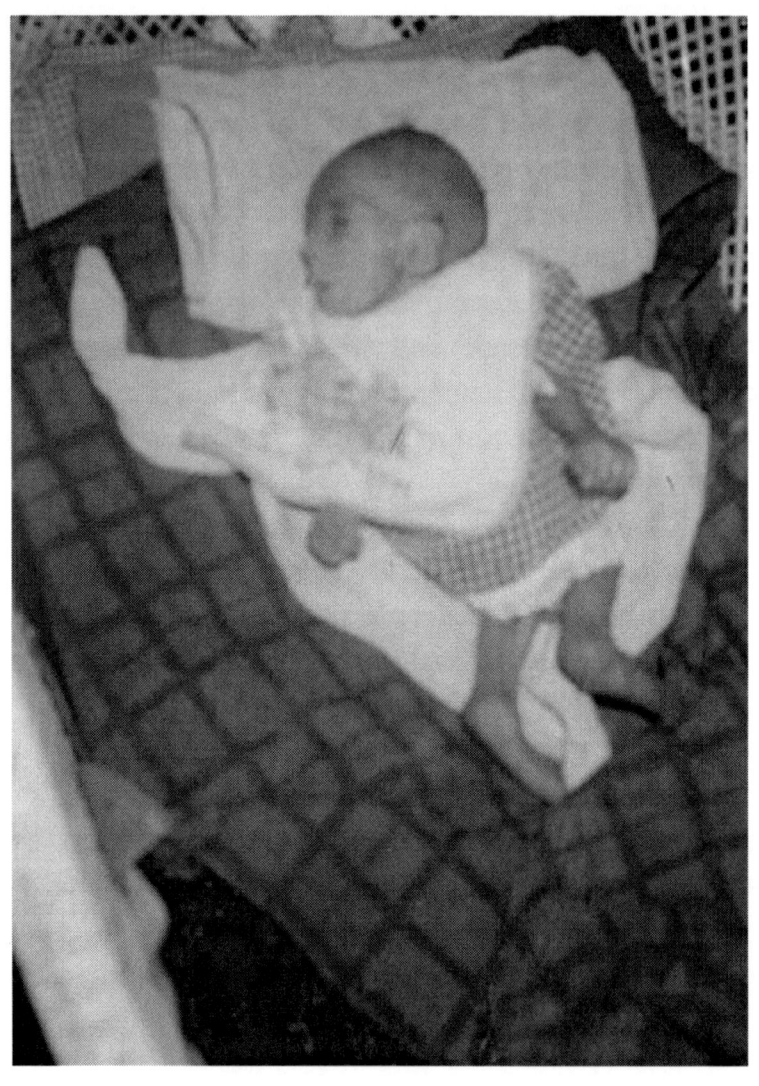

loyalty to his mother that I found so touching.

Mother Teresa says, 'Let us preach to you without preaching. Not by words, but by your example.' This is truly the essence of her work.

Later I learnt that the Sisters' vocation for prayer, contemplation, meditation and inner silence, was even more important than the life of service. This was why you always saw them looking relaxed and refreshed. They bubbled with a fountain of inner joy. The Sisters had been chosen for their laughter and happy spirits and I noticed that the centres were always filled with their humour. Indian people have a gift for joy, and these missionaries of charity were a beautiful reflection of this. Their faces and eyes shone with happiness and I never saw any who were 'burnt out' or depressed. They had been taught how to spiritually recharge their batteries. It was a far cry from my idea of embittered frustrated nuns that I had heard so much about from friends going through a convent education.

Each time I met Mother Teresa she said something as she passed. She was tiny in stature but her charisma was enormous.
She said to me,

'Love more everyday, love until it hurts, nothing less will do.' These words have influenced me greatly. And I often recall them in my present work with the dying.

Often she said, 'God is love – and he loves you and me. Let us love others as he loves us.'

Every day there were so many meetings, so many unique experiences. In a Delhi Centre I met an old woman who had been brought up by bears in the Himalayas. She was unable to use her vocal chords to speak, but she appeared content. She had difficulty walking and much preferred to crawl. She was beautifully and compassionately cared for. She loved to be massaged. Perhaps this felt like the bears washing her. I met her with a friend of mine. He had a thick beard. This thrilled her, and she kept stroking it. Perhaps too, this brought back the memory of bears' fur.

Then there was little Raju at Shishu Bhavan, the children's home in Calcutta. An eight-year old boy with TB meningitis. He needed to be constantly nursed and loved, to bring him out of an autistic condition.

In Delhi there was a baby who I named 'little monkey,' because she was no bigger than a baby monkey and just as wizened. Holding her dying body was one of the greatest privileges I have ever known. By loving her I felt I could love all those other children too weak or starved to fight for life. To me it felt like meeting the whole world. These experiences in India and Nepal made me think of all of humanity; all those who can never be reached except in your heart and thoughts.

Every day there were so many experiences, so many eyes that spoke silently, so many sores and wounds and emaciated bodies. Strangely I never felt sad because the peace, love and communication that I saw were greater than the sadness. They died gently. Afterwards they were laid in their sheets with honour and dignity. I felt that this was living and dying as it should be.

In Delhi there was a baby who I called the 'Ski Baby.' She had been born without feet, but she was about to be adopted by a Swiss couple. I felt sure that she would be fitted with false feet and would soon be shooting down the ski slopes of Switzerland as fast as the other children. I saw many couples collecting the babies they were adopting. They came from America, Switzerland, Germany, and Belgium. It was wonderful to see their faces when they met their long awaited child and gradually got to know them. At first they just fed and changed them. Then gradually they would take them to their hotels for a night or two. After a few days the babies and toddlers would cling to them as if they had always been together. One seven-year old boy told me very proudly, in English, that he had a mummy and daddy waiting for him in Italy.

In Nepal I cuddled a little girl of eighteen months who was recovering from TB. I remember her particularly because she clung to me frantically, needing the contact so badly. She had huge sad eyes in her emaciated face, with stick-like arms and legs and a swollen belly. Each time I had to put her down, she would huddle in a corner with tear filled eyes, looking like a little old woman. She couldn't bear the parting, and her little puckered face still haunts my memory.

Another memory that stands out is being invited by a father, in Katmandu, to stand by a burning pyre beside the holy river. The family stayed by the pyre for the three hours it took to burn the

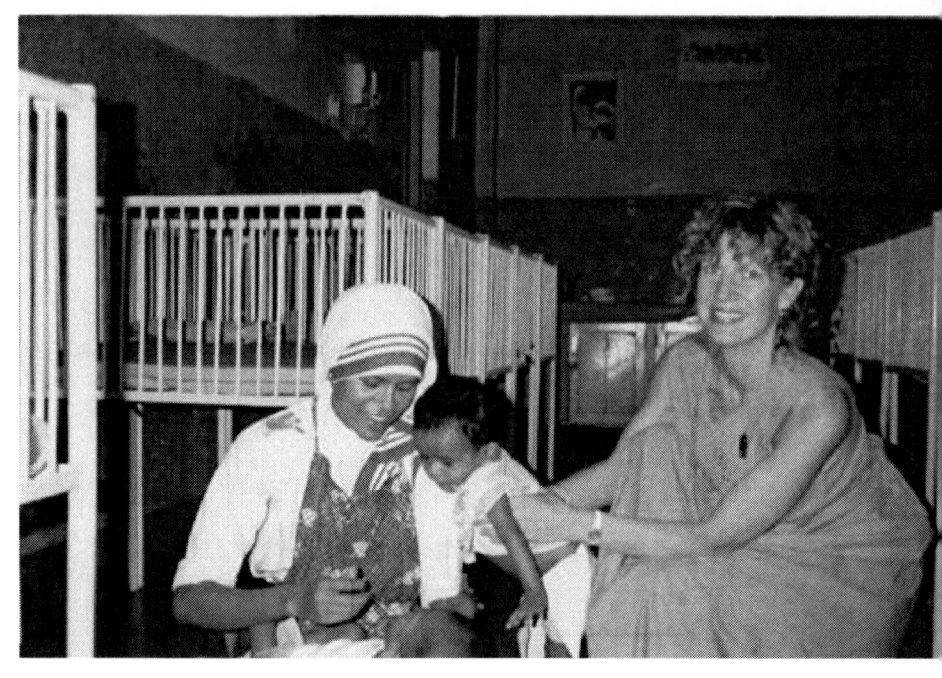

body. Lying by it was the little white shrouded body of an eight-year old boy. His father told me how the evening before he had been taken to hospital at six o'clock with dysentery and at six in the morning he was dead. There was a stunned shock and pain in his eyes, but he fought back the tears because he believed that crying holds the body back on the soul's journey. He said that the women in his family weren't allowed to come to the funeral because they couldn't control their grief. All the time they were building the pyre, the little black haired child lay shrouded. A child that yesterday had been playing. It was impossible not to share in his grief when he had been so open with me, a foreigner.

It filled me with awe to think, that here, they can accept life as it is, without resistance. Life for them is in the hands of God. They believe in an afterlife, and that faith is unwavering despite the pain and shock of the grief they experience.

For me, personally, the whole experience of holding, loving, comforting, embracing, and cradling these people, has redirected my life in some new inner way.

Volunteers are asked to come to India with a 'clean heart – a heart to love and hands to serve.' We did our best, but we were given back much, much more. Visiting the 'Mother House' where Mother Teresa and her Sisters live was a great experience. It was such a tranquil place. At six a.m. in the mornings, friends and I used to walk through the back streets, which were for once silent, on the way to the 'Mother

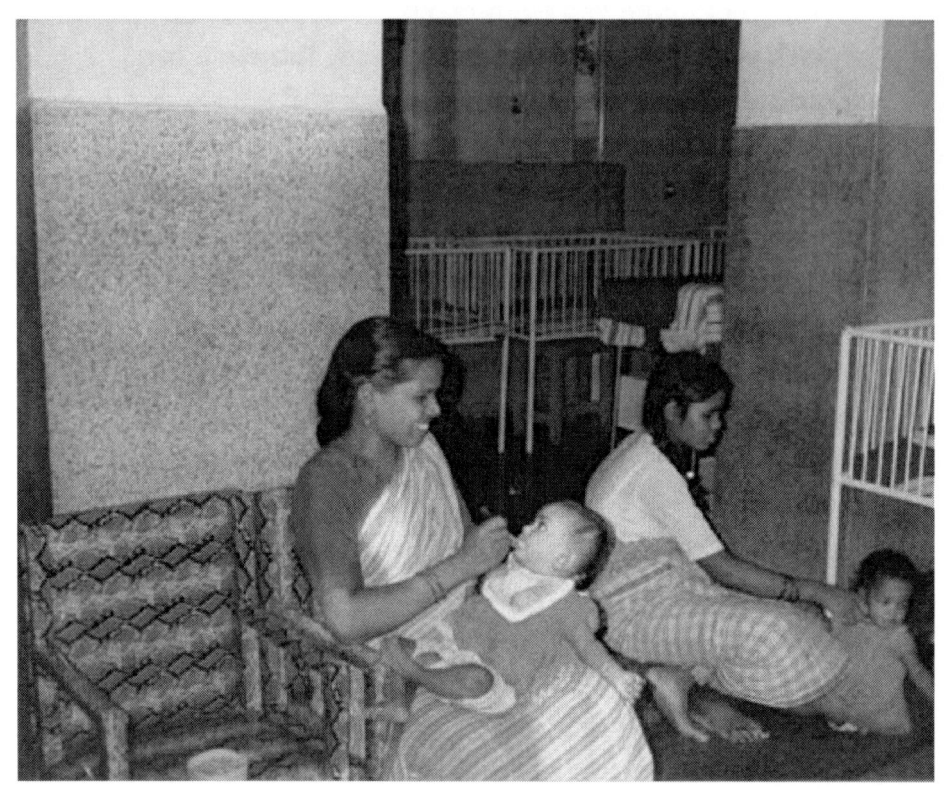

House' for early morning mass followed by tea with one of the Sisters. It was delightfully cool at this time, and the streets still had sleeping people scattered on the ground. The city was gradually stirring to life. The Sisters knelt as they chanted their mass before an altar with the words, 'I thirst.'

Above the soft chanting voices the sounds of Calcutta, roaring to life, entered the glassless windows. I used to gaze at Mother Teresa's beautiful hands, as they were held out in worship. Those loving, gnarled, used hands that had touched so many and coped with such arduous work.

Even now, eight years later, I often find myself transported back in my mind to the enveloping soothingness of this house. It has become a haven for my thoughts.

One sad memory of Calcutta was that of a handicapped man used for begging by a syndicate. Children were often brutally mutilated so that they could be used for begging. This young man was laid out at noon, the hottest time, on the pavement of a main street. He was deprived of liquid and his whole body palpitated in the raging heat. He lay in a pool of his sweat. Each day I used to empty my bottle of, by now, warm water over his head and buy him lemon water. I tried to prop him up to drink. He would gulp down the liquid, and look into my eyes and try to smile.

Whilst flying to Delhi from Calcutta, I sat by a professor who lived in Calcutta. He asked me why I was there. While telling him about the Centres, something made me mention this syndicated beggar. The professor

TB Centre in Katmandu, Nepal

bowed to me with his hands over his heart, in the 'nemesti' greeting, and said to me, 'You have come to India to help my people. In return for that help, I promise you, that when I return to Calcutta I will find this man. I will use my position to have him removed from the syndicate and taken to Mother Teresa.' He then asked me to describe the exact location where this man could be found.

I will never know if this happened, but I like to think this story had a happy ending.

Summer 1987

Be only all for
Jesus
through Mary.
Be holy.

God bless you
ec. Teresa mc

Mother Teresa in the background, Kilburn, London

PLASTIC BAGS IN THE CATHEDRAL

Saturday 25th October 2003

I stood at the back clutching my invitation, awed by the crowd. It had started earlier than the time on my invitation, but it didn't seem to matter. Far to the front the echoing voice of Cardinal Murphy O'Connor clearly reached me through speakers. In front of me were two blue and white sari-ed figures complete with the navy cardigans and black lace up shoes, which stood for winter wear. In spite of the cold they were looking as bright and radiantly cheerful as they always did. My memory flew back down the years – back to the times when I had last been with them.

The address over, I sidled forward. I'd spotted an empty seat with plastic bags piled around it. I slid into the vacant place and the old familiar odour of alcohol and unwashed bodies assailed me immediately. For no reason this touched a nerve, and tears of emotion pricked my eyes. Behind me a mumbling voice muttered oaths and threats.

'I'll f…ing knock his head in.' He muttered sadly to himself. No one minded. No one tut-tutted or turned their heads in disapproval. All heads were focussed on the front and the echoing, slightly disembodied voice of Cardinal O'Connor.

Next to me, a homeless man who later told me he was called Michael, beamed his joy, and stalwortly sung the responses on the sheets we had been handed at the door. My mind floated back to Calcutta, back to that voice and face that we were now celebrating. We, meaning those who had admired her so much. These people were those who she believed in, those she had dedicated her life to. The men around me had left their beer cans untouched, their faces rapt in pride. They were here to celebrate the much-loved life of a friend. It was the life of someone who had left a treasured mark on their lives, a person who they had trusted. The building was filled. Every age and nationality was there from all walks of life. Surely this was how Jesus had meant it to be. There were no barriers. All were united in her words of love. This day was a thanksgiving for the beatification of Mother Teresa in Westminster Cathedral.

Outside the door the homeless who hated coming into buildings, had gathered, still in sleeping bags to shut out the frosty cold. Soon they too were to be blessed by Cardinal O'Connor. He would touch their heads and faces just as Mother Teresa would have done. My heart melted with inner tears. This somehow seemed to be the reality of her life and teachings. All the shops and bright lights of London seemed this day to be out of place. It was as if only the spirit that was here mattered.

Somehow the thousands squeezed into the

Cathedral filed out; many of them to go and have refreshments in the hall next door. It was like the feeding of the five thousand. There were enough sandwiches and tea for everyone who needed them. The Indian families hastily grabbed chairs. They wanted front seats for their families to see a film of the funeral of Mother Teresa. It reminded me of flying Air India when the Indian families, as soon as they were aboard, grabbed all the pillows and blankets while the other passengers were still stowing their belongings in the lockers. In this hall now, their plates were piled with sandwiches. I sipped at my tea. I'd only taken crisps, as I'd guiltily wondered how many homeless people had helped make the sandwiches with the sisters. As in previous years I'd worked as a volunteer in the homeless hostel in Kilburn and was a bit too aware of the lack of hygiene.

Then the film that had been made by the Pettie family began. There on the screen was the remarkable face of 'Mother' talking in the special way that only she could talk. Then the story of her death in1997 narrated by the sisters who had been at her side. Afterwards her funeral was shown. It seemed as if the whole of Calcutta had filed by her body to say their farewells. She lay in an open coffin looking so like herself. The service was in a football stadium with Muslims, Hindus, Jains, Christians, Buddhists, Jews, and Prime Ministers from many countries as well as Royalty. No doubt Princess Diana would have represented Britain if she had not died the very same week.

The coffin was paraded through the streets, mourned by rich and poor alike. Tears were running down some people's cheeks. She had brought all the multi faiths together that day, all united in her teaching of love. Her words whispered in my mind in that wonderful Albanian-Indian accented voice of hers,

'It doesn't matter how much you do, it is the love that you do it with that matters.'

I thought back to that time in 1987 to the centre for the dying in Calcutta, and the joy I had experienced at being there when I had worked as a volunteer with Mother Teresa. Here she was on film being taken back from the stadium to her home in the Mother House. She was carried on a gun carriage, which was the way that India could honour her the most. She was laid in the floor of the courtyard, and all the sisters, alone with her now, dropped sand and flower petals onto the coffin. She really would be with them always, physically and spiritually. They felt she was watching over them all, still loving them in death as she had loved and cherished them in life. Outside the army fired guns in her honour.

In the Cathedral, Michael, the homeless man sitting on my right had gone up arm and arm with me for a blessing, while the Catholic people took communion.

'We lost two great ladies together' he'd muttered, still slightly inebriated. 'Mother Teresa and Diana.
Did you know that Cardinal O'Connor could be the next Pope?'

I'd replied that I didn't know, and we'd smiled at each other in happy sharing of the information.

I saw no one I recognized. The sisters I'd worked with in London in the 1980s had long since moved to other countries, but I returned back to that time in my thoughts and remembered the sharing and unique times that we had together while living and working in the Kilburn Hostel with the homeless. As my thoughts turned back to Calcutta, I again felt emotionally moved. I felt so at home with all of this and very deeply affected. It was one of those great moments of connection that we have in life. The connection with their lives, their love and their purpose. Purpose in that spiritual way is something I have lost since those times. I have only had rare glimpses of it. Perhaps it is the loss of that simplicity. Perhaps it is the material life and the concerns that sweep me away, but whatever it is I do know that Mother Teresa's life and work was very close to Christ, and Jesus becomes very real when I am where Mother Teresa and her sisters and co-workers are. It is life that is faith in action. Perhaps I feel I belong here because I can show my emotions and feelings without fear of being despised. I look back to my time cradling the dying, stroking the faces of those with leprosy who had no feeling in their hands and those beautiful children in the orphanages. As I remember 'Mother's' remarkable gnarled hands cradling the handicapped, the malformed, the demented elderly person, the child I too can feel the love that filled me. This is what poured into my heart as I sat as a guest in Westminster

Cathedral surrounded by dignitaries and the homeless. This is what I feel when I work with drug offenders, giving them relaxation and meditation in a beautiful candlelit space. Then I remember that reassuring voice of Mother Teresa when she used to walk past me,

'Love more every day. Love 'till it hurts.'

PHYLLIS MARY HARVEY

My mother, Phyllis Mary Harvey (nee Bailey) was born in Bath in 1916. She went to the Hermitage House School and kept up a life-long contact with the friends she made there.

Phyllis had many talents. As a young girl she cycled far around the Conkwell lanes at Winsley. She loved the countryside and this inspired her to write poetry and children's stories. Phil, as she was known to her friends, was a keen naturalist and ornithologist and this was something she passed on to her children and grandchildren.

Each spring she knew where every nest was being built in the garden at 'Linleys'. She taught the children to identify the eggs and fledglings. Many family holidays were spent in Devon, North Wales and Cornwall, and there are many photos to be found of seagull eggs.

In later life, Phyllis was thrilled to have badgers and foxes coming to her garden door. Always a keen photographer, she will be remembered by her children as lining them up for poses on holidays.

She was a lady with green fingers. Her garden at Linleys flourished under her care, as did all the homegrown vegetables, strawberries and fruits. Her borders were a gardener's dream, and annually the flowers seemed to multiply. The blooms often appeared in her clever flower arrangements.

She was also a talented home decorator, always keeping one step ahead of the damp patches.

Phyllis was expert with all the family pets. As a child she had loved her Spaniel. During her marriage she had three Alsatians, a Labrador and two Great Danes, as well as numerous family cats and kittens, hamsters, mice, guinea-pigs, rabbits, the odd slow worm, hedgehogs and sick birds introduced by her children. She always had cardboard boxes at hand for the latest batch of kittens, or a sick animal. Also, she was always ready to help with pet funerals.

She also joined in with her daughter's ponies. It was Phyllis who always managed to catch Fred, when everybody else had failed. This she did even though horses gave her hay fever.

Her gentleness was recognised by animals and children. She had a great ability to enter into the world of youngsters.

As a young girl she had helped out on a children's ward. The young patients used to call her 'The Beautiful White Lady.' Perhaps she might have nursed if she hadn't married, and had her own four children. These nursing days were happy memories for Phyllis.

A keen tennis player, she was known for her formidable underarm serve and two-handed backhand. She met her husband Eric at a tennis party, at the Sutcliffe House, which was then a private house and is now a hospice known as 'Dorothy House'.

They were married for over 50 years and had a long and happy marriage until his death in 1985.

Phyllis was a great walker and naturalist. This she enjoyed with her husband Eric, children and grandchildren, always accompanied by a dog. She also loved ballet, theatre and musicals, and in later years always took her grandchildren to the Bath pantomime.

She was an excellent cook, and was able to turn out meals for large groups of family and friends. She always had a houseful for Christmas.

Although not a golf player herself, she regularly accompanied Eric to Sham Castle while he played, and enjoyed the bird life while she was there.

Bridge was another of Phyllis's talents, and she continued this until recently.

She was always a loyal friend, and a great source of spiritual strength in time of need. She was close to her sisters-in-law, Betty and Prue, and went on family holidays with them to Cornwall, often with grandchildren too. Cornwall, she said, was her 'spiritual home' where she felt 'closest to heaven', staying in a cottage overlooking the sea at Rock.

She was a loving grandmother and she and Eric often had grandchildren visiting and staying. She took a keen interest in them all. She had eight in number which she was very proud of.

Phil's life was a long and rich one. Through happiness and hardship she never lost her faith and love of beauty. Those who knew her will remember the flowers that filled her home, and her love of nature and gardens, the sea and open spaces. Above all she will be remembered for her gentleness, her kind and thoughtful nature, and her patience.

Phyllis's life has truly been well lived.

Phyllis Mary Harvey, nee Bailey, 1916-1996

George Frederick Hammond with his son Eric

IT'S NEVER TOO LATE

'Mummy who's that man over there?'

Puzzled, my eyes followed his finger. He was showing me an old blurred sepia photograph, squeezed amongst cards and wooden animals on the mantelpiece. I paused before replying, thinking, Yes who was this man?

'It's your Great Grandfather.'

'Do I know him?' said Joel.

'No, he died many years ago in the First World War.'

'What's his name?'

'I don't know'.

'Why don't you know, Mummy?'

'Yes,' I thought, 'why don't you know?' Provoked by my six-year-old's questions I looked closely at the photograph. It seemed tragic not to know. Here was a tall long legged man, riding a large tricycle, with a little cart attached, holding a three year old child not unlike the blonde curly-haired boy that my son had been at the same age.

The child was my father Eric looking serious while his soldier dad was taking him for a ride. The man was wearing a formal suit of the period of the First World War. Even blurred, he looked astonishingly like my own father had looked as a young man. The same tight, coarse, crinkly curls, the same upright stance and long legs that made him over six feet in height.

My own parents had died, my mother very recently, which is how this photo had come to be in my hands. With it had come the one remaining card that this father had written to his baby son, written from the front.

It read, in capitals:

'DEAR ERIC,
I HOPE YOU ARE BEING A GOOD BOY AND LOOKING AFTER YOUR MUMMY? I HOPE TO SEE YOU VERY SOON.
                    LOVE FROM YOUR DADDY'.

I had first placed this photo out on Remembrance Sunday the year before and there it had stayed. This forgotten man, unknown to all the family. It was only as an adult that I discovered that the beloved Grandpa I had known all my life was actually my step Grandfather. He had married my Grandmother May and adopted her two sons Eric, who was four and baby Geoffrey. Then it had been a closely kept secret that the boys had a different father killed in the war. Only after Grandpa had died were we able to mention this unknown soldier. Both his boys were very like him to look at.

Strangely, at the time I put the photo out

different members of the family were also thinking about him. None of us had talked to each other about it. We were all individually prompted. Peter, one of my cousins changed his surname from Harvey, to HAMMOND the surname of this Grandparent. Then Penny, my eldest brother's wife began a search for his details and suddenly the photograph had an identity.

His name was GEORGE FREDERICK HAMMOND. He was born in ILFORD, ESSEX. He married May in 1911 at the age of 26. I clearly remember my Grandmother telling me how she played the piano and sang songs to her suitors in her mother's drawing room, so it was here that George had courted and won her for his wife. They then married and moved to Westbury Road, Ilford, where my father and his younger brother were born.

George, who was a metal dealer's clerk, joined the army in Ilford in the Cycling Corps. Perhaps that is why my father had been introduced to cycling so early. Certainly our family had a great aptitude for sports. We know that his army number was 20669. Somehow this information made George a real person.

After the battle of the Somme so many soldiers were killed that George was moved from the Ilford Essex Regiment to be a replacement in the Warwickshire Regiment. He was then a Signaller. His last battle was at Bullecourt, just south of Arras in France. The research showed that on that day the British and the French had an offensive and were pushing forwards to recover ground. George met his death very early in the morning. The signalling lamp was shelled and we assume him with it. Two thirds of the men were killed with him. It was some time later before the bodies could be recovered and there in France is a mass grave for those tragic, brave men who died.

The name George Frederick Hammond lies on a remembrance stone in France, and in a specially built chapel for the 2000 Ilford men who died in the Great War. His name is also recorded in a memorial for the Warwickshire Regiment in that county.

It has taken more than eighty years for George to be openly mourned, thought about and remembered by his offspring, but it is happening now. At last I can say to my son:

'This is your Great Grandfather George Frederick. He was a very kind brave man who loved cycling like you, and took your Grandfather as a baby in a bike cart, just like I took you on the back of a bike and in a cart down the canal path. Your Great Grandfather is buried at Bullecourt in France.'

Perhaps my Grandfather can now feel cared about. His two sons had six children between them, five boys and one girl. There are eight great grand-children. In all of them you see the Hammond physique, the long legs, the thick hair and the promise of tallness. So George has lived on in his children and grand-children and great grand-children, even when we were all unaware he existed.

My Grandmother May must have kept her grief hidden. She re-married 19 months after his death and was able to bring her children out of foster care where she'd had to put them after being widowed, while she earned money to keep them in Exeter, then meeting her next husband there.

I will always wonder how much George suffered in that terrible, cruel, meaningless war, where so many men had to put themselves forward to be slaughtered. The little son Eric in the cart also grew up to be a soldier in the Second World War, where he received the Military Cross for bravery. Happily his life was spared, and he came back to enjoy his family and my twin brother and I were born after the war.

So George, eighty-one years on, we thank you for all that your life meant. Now you can be a person, as well as GEORGE FREDERICK HAMMOND, NUMBER 20669 of the WARWICKSHIRE REGIMENT, who will be remembered from the one photograph as always young.

Joel and Kayleigh

FAREWELL TO AUNT ALICE

Aunt Alice loved life. I can see her now; romping round the tennis court with her formidable underarm serve, driving much too fast round country lanes.

'Shut your eyes,' she used to snap at her nervous passengers, 'I've never hit anything yet.'

She gave me my first driving lessons in the Welsh mountains. I might have been underage, but ever since hill starts and hairpin beds have given me no difficulties.

Auntie drove ambulances in the war, sailed boats in all weathers, rode the toughest horses and climbed mountains. But dinner parties and entertaining would make her flap like a sheet in the wind.

Her large trestle table would be moved round the room and the chairs rearranged many times while the place settings were altered. Would Colonel Brown like Major Johns? Would Mrs Havering mix with Arnold Watts? It was exhausting to watch, but ultimately the dinners were a great success.

It came as quite a shock when Aunt Alice died. She seemed to take her last illness totally in her stride. She mastered it as she did her horses, and as she took her last breath she seemed to say,

'Thank God I've got that over.'

It was left to me to organise her funeral. I told myself that I should see this as a new life experience. There must be a first time for everything.

I managed the registration of the death certificate, although as I watched her name being inscribed in beautiful italics in that everlasting book I couldn't help wondering if I had spelt her maiden name correctly. I was under oath. I had always known her by her married name, White.

As I left the office feeling slightly guilty, I could picture Auntie giving a snort:

'Why make a fuss over a spelling?'

Then a new picture filled my mind – Alice's dinner parties – perhaps she would panic about it. With this amusing picture, the worry left me.

My next hurdle was the visit to the undertaker. Mr Gordon Wells had assured me on the telephone that they had been a family business for over forty years.

'Your Auntie is very well looked after,' he assured me. 'I am going to work on her tomorrow, and you can see her any time after two o'clock. We only use old fashioned methods here.'

I swallowed. I could hear my voice sounding higher as I squeaked,

'I've never seen anybody prepared; only when they've…um…just died.'

'My dear,' soothed the voice, in a well-oiled way, used to its overwhelmed, grieving clients. 'Auntie will look very different. You'll see.'

He then briefed me about all the formalities and I agreed to go the next afternoon to sign the necessary papers. On the day of the visit, it snowed.

'Perhaps it will be too bad to drive over,' I thought hopefully.

Alas, the sun shone. I built a snowman with the children and, looking at the roads outside, I saw they were clear. My husband packed me off. At least I didn't have to take the children.

I arrived still in my bobble hat and scarf; red nosed from our snowball fights. Mr Wells met me, looking impeccable in his dark black suit. He shook my hand firmly – his felt cold. It seemed that he was looking askance at my appearance, so I mumbled that I'd come from building a snowman. I'm sure I saw an eyebrow raised.

'Now my dear, would you like to see your dear Auntie first, or discuss a little paperwork?'

Oh no! I thought, I'll really have to see Alice now, he's gone to so much trouble 'doing her'. Someone has to make it worthwhile for all his efforts.

'Umm, I think I'd like to do the paperwork first,' I said, thinking that I might have to make a quick exit.

After I had settled myself with a number of formal signings, he sat back in his chair.

'Now I have one little worry,' he said. 'Auntie's hair. I think her parting falls on the left side,' he gestured. 'Does this seem right to you, my dear, or would you like me to alter it?'

My eyes dilated. 'No, no, I'm sure her hair will

be perfect as you have done it,' I swallowed.

The moment could be put off no longer. He was about to lead me to the Chapel of Rest.

Mr Wells was a tall thin man. I couldn't guess his age. Perhaps he was in his sixties. What I couldn't get over was the look of his eyes. They must have been black, but I swear they had a film over them.

'Don't be silly,' I told myself. 'He's probably got cataracts.'

But still I wondered if working for years with the dead made you take on the appearance of your clients.

We had arrived. Mr Wells took out a key and unlocked the chapel door. It was a tiny room and in front of me was the coffin. I saw two marble white hands clasped together.

'Is that Mrs White?' I asked.

'Of course. Come in my dear. There she is.'

I forced my eyes to look, peering from a safe position behind the undertaker.

'Oh, I'd no idea,' I said, as I saw beautiful frills around the edge of the coffin, and Alice in a satin gown with a lace neck.

The coffin was tastefully decorated like a baby's Moses basket. Somehow I had imagined she would be in a hospital nightie. Then I saw her face. Mr Wells was right. Old or new-fashioned ways, she looked quite different from in the hospital. I noticed how delicately applied her make up was. In fact, she looked peaceful and so young. Yes, even the hair with the dreaded left parting was done attractively.

'Oh, she looks lovely!' I gasped, really impressed.

She still held, folded in her hands, the flower the devoted hospital nurses had put there.

'Your job really is a work of art.'

He bowed his grey head, looking gratified.

I then departed. It surprised me that so much trouble goes into this pursuit of excellence that quite often is never witnessed.

I arrived home to a warming tea of toasted crumpets with the children. I thought back nostalgically to my childhood, when Aunt Alice would let me toast crumpets on a toasting fork before her open fire, after long country walks. Alice was alive in my thoughts. Already I was remembering her again as vibrant and youthful. There were so many good memories to bridge her loss.

A SUMMER IN THE LIFE OF BALLYMURPHY

There is a long tapering hill, crowned by rugged mountains. White granite houses to the right, fronting a large housing estate. Wasteland to the left, with a rectangular library and youth centre planted amidst the glass and rubble. Burnt our cars. Wire fences half unravelled, wire which is used for stretching across the road in front of army tanks called 'Pigs'. Lamp posts, one in particular for the tarring and feathering. Treacherous stray dogs. Children in abundance, toddlers to teenagers. Harassed mothers, some husbands in Long Kesh prison. Teenage boys, quick to throw stones when they feel threatened. Youths smoking, trying to show a veneer of toughness to hide their vulnerability. Black taxicabs that covered Turf Lodge, Ballymurphy and the Falls Road: 10p a ride to Belfast centre, stopping like a bus to pick up passengers. Irish music played in the clubs. Adults and children ever ready to sing a song, dance a jig, or play the haunting music of Ireland.

This conjures up my memories of Ballymurphy in Belfast, where I lived the summer of 1973 with a team of students. We ran a play scheme in the community centre as part of a plan to keep children off the streets, away from any trouble.

Ballymurphy is a Catholic area and at this time it was at the height of the troubles in Northern Ireland. When violence was about to happen in the area there was an invisible but tangible atmosphere you could feel like a vibration. People retreated into their houses and the streets emptied. Then, inevitably, there would be a bomb scare or a shooting. Ballymurphy gave me a wealth of experience. I loved the local people and the children were some of the most creative I had worked with. As they live with so much cruel reality in their lives, they love fairy tales and make believe – 'happily ever after.'

One double event stands out starkly in my memory, as I faced near death. There had been a shooting at the top of Ballymurphy. I had heard the gun shots, but my friends and I thought it was all over, so we were ready to go down to the centre of Belfast to play music with friends. We stopped a black taxi and, clutching our instruments, we all five of us piled in. Unknown to us however, we were being watched by army binoculars.

They had decided we were responsible for the shooting and the guns were hidden in our instrument cases. They had built a road block near the bottom of the hill, before it led onto the Falls Road. The soldiers were there waiting, guns at the ready, in case the taxi decided to crash the barricade. In Ballymurphy there was no garage. All cars were serviced by locals, and the brakes of this taxi were unreliable when it came to emergency stops on a hill. I clearly remember the taxi braking and sliding towards the barriers while seeing one particular gun pointed towards my forehead. I was in the front seat. It all seemed like slow motion as I watched the soldier's finger tighten on the trigger, one eye closed, the other looking through the sight. If we crashed through that bullet was for me. Mercifully, we slid to a halt against the barrier and that finger lifted, although the rifles still pointed at us. We were hustled out of the taxi with the inevitable jabbing of weapons in our stomachs and backs.

The soldiers were as shaken as we were. They too must have thought we were going to let go with machine gun fire as we crashed through the barriers. They looked so young. They made us lean against the car and roughly frisked us in army fashion, before searching the instrument cases for shorn-off shotguns, grenades and machine guns. Only then did they relax gruffly to send us on our way. We were six trembling people, including the taxi driver.

I think the greatest lesson I learnt in these Northern Ireland experiences was how fear leads people to immediate aggression as a defence. Those unfortunate soldiers were brutal, due to the reaction after fear. The children were quick to hurl a stone after any criticism. I saw young children pulling the legs off a frog in the mountains, because it frightened them when it jumped.

Once we reached Belfast we went to our party in a Protestant area to play our music. Hardly any time had passed before there was a violent hammering on the door, followed by a few hard kicks, which burst the flimsy door open. We stared in horror as two burley men rushed in, brandishing guns and threatening to shoot us if we played any more 'Catholic' music. Shaken and numb with this second shock of the evening, we retreated back to Ballymurphy, glad to be alive and unhurt. Each day produced some new drama.

That night, my mattress on the floor seemed very welcoming, even though it was sodden with cat pee. This had admittedly kept it free of bedbugs, and although this had been very hard to live with a week ago, it had become trivial after a week spent in Ballymurphy.

Summer 1974

GUNS AND BOMBS

I've always been a timid person. I remember as a child being put by my parents on a train going to London and all the way being terrified that my Grandmother wouldn't be there to meet me, thinking that I'd be lost forever. I can still remember that feeling of terror that only an eight-year-old can feel.

But now I was facing fear everyday in Northern Ireland. Strangely, when there is something tangible to fear, it is easier than those imaginary anxieties which collect in the mind. Each day is enhanced, and life becomes very intense, joyful and precious when you know it could be your last. Everything is heightened. The events I am thinking about happened in Londonderry in Northern Ireland in the 1970s.

I was staying there with a group of students doing projects for the Baha'i Faith, including being part of the street play schemes. We had a centre in the middle of the city on a steep hill just by the city gates. This particular day we were here with a group of students. There were youths from both Catholic and Protestant areas with us, which is probably why the event which happened next came about.

Suddenly the door burst open, and a young man of about eighteen crashed into the room, brandishing a gun and yelling at us to get back against the wall with our hands up, which we did. I remember feeling amazed rather than frightened, it was so unexpected. He was shaking with fear and the gun pointed at us was shaking too. He started to talk,

'I'm Junior IRA. I've shot people and I'm going to shoot you too.'

I remember thinking that this guy must have had a break-down. He then proceeded to tell us who he had shot and why. All the time his hands shook, and I remember thinking,

'O God, the gun is going to go off by mistake in those trembling hands.'

Minutes past as we let him talk himself out. Really it was his grief, shock and horror at what he had done. Finally, when he was spent, we talked gently back to him, never moving from the wall and he slowly calmed. We persuaded him that he had nothing to fear from us, and that Baha'is were about unity, not conflict, and he and the gun finally left.

The most terrifying events were the bombs. Occasionally there would be a bomb warning, and every part of me just wanted to run blindly. But there was a problem: you never knew in which direction to run. Inevitably there would be two separate blasts so which way was safety? On this particular occasion I was on the hill near the Baha'i Centre building. Sirens sounded and army tanks drove past me with loud speakers telling us to clear the area and warn others. I knew that the building where our centre was had many different offices inside. Fighting the urge to flee, I had to force myself to enter the building. I raced up the stairs and banged on every door shouting,

'Leave the building, leave the building – Bomb scare!'

I still recall the rasping sound of my panicked breathing. I was so terrified I remember being numb when the terror turns into a disassociated, blank state. Only then could I leave the building and run, run, run. There were two blasts, one shortly followed by the second. Luckily, they were not close to me. I had chosen the right direction to flee. I can't describe the explosion or the impact. The ground shakes, everything rattles and the noise fills your head and reverberates on and on. Those who are too close can suffer slipped retinas and perforated eardrums. Even now, when I hear an unexpected shot, or an explosive sound, something freezes in me preparing myself for flight.

It is the same with gun-shots. I worked on play buses that drove all over Belfast to Catholic and Protestant troubled areas to take the small children off the streets. This was work I loved. At this period I was training to be a teacher at Winchester, and I worked in Northern Ireland in my holidays as I was writing a thesis on the effects of the troubles on children. A few times there were gun shots in the area and immediately we got the children onto the floor of the bus, and shielded as many of them as we could with our own bodies. They thought this was a game as we had rehearsed it. We had one two-year-old whose father had been shot while lying on her to protect her, so it was a real danger. Even today, a rifle shot or an unexpected firework will make me want to flatten my body onto the ground, even though consciously I know there is no threat.

As well as Belfast I also spent time in Strabane. Here we had to knock on doors to collect children for a play scheme. The Irish hospitality, involving strong tar-filled tea and biscuits, was immense. When they realised I was an English student they would bring out their trophies for me to admire. These usually consisted of painted white handkerchiefs. The ones I best remember were gun sites aimed at soldiers' heads. There was no malice in this. I don't think any connection was made between me, as an English student helping their children to stay off the dangerous streets, and the soldiers.

Another close call happened in Ballymurphy. Two English soldiers on patrol came into the play scheme centre. Hearing I was English, they smiled at me and asked where I was from. It was such an innocent thing. Then to our horror the children started chanting:

'Julie's going out with an English soldier… Julie's going out with an English soldier!'

The soldiers retreated, and I shook with fear. I had that awful shaking feeling of disaster. I thought I would be shot. I thank God to this day that I wasn't. These children who daily faced horrible events were always unpredictable.

One day, the group of volunteers I worked with and I took the children down to the Falls Road, to the local baths to go swimming. It was a public holiday and the baths turned out to be closed. The group of forty children began to riot, throwing everything they could find as a protest. All we could do was to gather up the little children and leave the rest of them to it. Nothing else could be done.

For me, personally, all this has taught me that, although I can often worry and be fearful, I do have an inner strength that I can draw on. It is possible for me to be brave in spite of the fear. After completing my thesis on Northern Ireland my tutor wrote at the end of his comments:

'An 'A' is deserved. – I am relieved that it did not have to be awarded posthumously!'

MIMOSA

February. There is mimosa on the street flower stall in Bath. I stop to gaze at the flowers as I do every year and I promise myself that I will buy a bunch to remember. Mimosa means to me my time living in Aix en Provence in the South of France.

This story began in 1970 when I was hitching with my Norwegian friend Ingunn through Provence. We were then au pairs living in Geneva. We were picked up by a retired French couple, Madame and Monsieur Dumas. They told us all about the history of Aix and took us back to their home for a meal. They promised to find us a room if we wanted to return to Aix at a later date to study French. After finishing in Geneva, working during the summer at a tomato nursery in Bath and then on Ingunn's parents'farm, picking carrots and cucumbers in Orre in Norway, we found ourselves the next September in our room in 9, Rue Aude, a room over a nougat factory which was part of a house owned by a very old couple who had been in the French Resistance.

This was an idyllic year. The Dumas's became our adopted parents. I taught English and studied French at the Foreign University for foreigners. It was a beautiful old frescoed building overlooking a courtyard of shady plane trees. Many a time my mind drifted from the lectures as I gazed out of the open windows to the trees full of chattering sparrows. This especially happened during the lectures on Rabelais. I studied, in French, sixteenth century, nineteenth century and twentieth century literature and this is how mimosa came into my life's experience. The scent still stays with me.

Every spring the orchards outside Aix are filled with mimosa. Monsieur Dumas took us to see these orchards. So, seeing mimosa in the flower stalls brings back the bliss of spring in Provence with the blue skies, singing birds and that heady, heady scent from those clumps of little round balls of yellow.

My writing started in Aix with poetry. I wrote and studied in the cafés, living on café au lait and croissants, and here I would write my French essays on Rabelais, Proust, Balzac and Flaubert. I loved to people-watch and read and read the novels of these authors, filling myself up with France in French.

Every morning I walked through the cobbled, narrow, ancient streets of Aix on the way to the university, stopping at the market for fresh bread, olives, pears and cherries. My staple diet came from this market. One stall holder, who became a friend, had a pet squirrel who sat on his shoulder. When I think of a romantic idyll I think of Aix and the walks on Cezanne's mountain, Saint Victoire. I remember dancing there in the early morning with the exaltation of being in such a beautiful place.

So since that time I have always written in cafes as I am doing today.

In memory of Anna Hinton, my dear friend in Aix and all those happy times, and of Ingunn and Monsieur and Madame Dumas, nos parents.

FEZ

The years roll back and I find my thoughts again in Morocco, The house where I stayed in Fez was with a Jewish family. I recall feeling very disturbed on our arrival to find the women of the house wailing, rocking and scratching their faces as a memorial to a son who had died the year before; this was the anniversary. I couldn't help wondering why they hadn't noticed the return of a living son, Joseph, who we travelled home with from Switzerland. What was my role as a guest? Should I have joined in the wailing with the women, or joined the men of the family? I never knew the correct answer. I joined the men. My Norwegian girlfriend and I had been invited to stay as guests of Joseph, the second son.

Jumbled memories stir. The glorious sunsets, one moment a ball of red fire in the sky; then a sudden darkness as the sun slid behind the mountains. The bustle and noise of the bazaars, the nauseating smell of the meat markets, white flesh crawling with flies; the hammering of the metal workers as they formed intricate patterns with their hammers and chisels; the dye vats on the roofs, with their cloying smells.

I remember the children, bare footed, vibrant, with their black eyes brimming with curiosity, trying out their power on the tourists. There were the gnarled, lined faces of the men, old before their years;

the sudden mystery of the ancient university, with its awe-inspiring Arab calligraphy and the haunting call to prayer from the mosques. The hidden magical courtyards with turquoise mosaic floors and singing fountains, secreted behind the dirty street doors, and the harmonious singsong of Arabic.

Above all I remember the hospitality, especially when visiting a Berber in an old stick hut at the back of a mountain village compound. He was a retired university professor who had come home to end his days in his village. He spoke fluent French. Nearly blind, he prepared green tea for us. He possessed only a sack for sleeping on, a teapot, some sticks for the fire, a dirt-incrusted tin cup, and a piece of dried up bread in a small dusty sack. Then he served it to us, yet when I resisted, saying how he must keep it, I recall the sound of his gentle voice speaking in French:

'Allah will provide,' he said with such a joyous smile.

I think of this lesson now as if it was yesterday. It was my first life's lesson in trust. So as I sipped the tea, and nibbled the bread brushing away the flies and dirt, I shared the feast, struggling with my western mistrust. How touched and honoured I felt to be sharing with this man, whilst at the same time hoping the water was properly boiled, and I wasn't going to get cholera from the dirt. Happily I didn't, so now I just think of the simplistic beauty of that experience.

There are many things from the Muslim culture that have had a profound effect on my understanding of life ever since.

Summer 1970

LIFE TO DIE

I am writing this article as a tribute to Columb, who achieved such a transition in the last days of his life. I also wish to acknowledge his parents who were there for his first breath and his last. They played a vital role in this story.

I first met Columb in November 1994. He had asked me to visit him in hospital, to help emotionally and spiritually. He knew he was in the last weeks of his life due to a brain tumour. He was a very honest person and faced what was now happening head on.

When I first came to know Col he was in deep anguish and fear. Being a person who loved communication with those near to him, he was afraid that the tumour would isolate him completely. He needed to be in control. Losing the ability to interact was his greatest dread.

Columb knew exactly what he wanted my role to be. Over the weeks we practised relaxation methods.

'Above all I want my heart to be opened and the ability to feel love again,' he told me.

Fear had blocked these feelings, and this had led to estrangements in his life amongst closest friends and family.

Terminal illness for such a young vital man had

naturally led to feelings of anger at life's treatment of him, and of those around him. It had been only too easy to push those dearest to him away. He now wanted to change all this.

Columb was perhaps the bravest person I have known. He was determined to break through all the barriers even though he knew this would be enormously painful.

He asked me, as a National Federation healer, to pray for him in those first weeks. He would reveal to me all the emotions and fears that caused his anguish, and I would pray out loud as he'd requested while he gently let himself drift into sleep. He was often exhausted as he kept himself awake day and night in dread of dying while he slept, or of the tumour taking over. Naturally as tiredness took hold he became increasingly troubled and disorientated. His exhausted body needed peaceful sleep more than anything.

One of the joys of knowing Col was his humour. Being Irish he was full of charm, and ever ready to crack a joke or make a cryptic remark, which would have everybody around him laughing away their grief. At times like this it was hard to recognise that he was dying. He was so in touch with life and all it meant.

When he first arrived in the hospital, he had alienated himself from his parents. As soon as they heard where he was they rushed to be near, and this time they were allowed to stay. Thus began the most moving relationship. They stayed in his bungalow five minutes away from the hospital and spent the rest of the time with him. During this period he was very distressed at being alone at night, so Mary, his mother, spent every night sitting with him in his room. She had only occasional times off, when a friend or a private nurse filled in for her.

During two months of these nights together they talked and talked, sharing everything that needed to be shared. Mary was able to experience, with her grown-up son, what few mothers are privileged to have: closeness. While she slept for a few hours in the day, Columb's father, Patrick, sat with him, only leaving the room when his many close friends dropped by. During this period, all that needed to be dealt with was healed in this honest closeness. The nurses and doctors on the ward were all moved by this selfless loving. One day Mary asked a Greek consultant doctor how much time was left.

'We can't say,' he said gently, 'but enjoy every moment you have with him.' He bowed and touched her compassionately on the arm.

Christmas came and went. The specialists had expected it all to be over before this time. Then New Year passed. Two of Columb's great friends, Celia and Peter, moved into the hospital with Mary and Patrick, to share sitting with him, doing different night and day shifts, so everybody could get some rest. There was a beautiful atmosphere in that side-room. It now had Columb's stamp on it.

A photograph of two dolphins flying above the waves stands out in my memory. To me, this symbolised the joy and freedom he was seeking on leaving his body. Nine years previously Seamus, Columb's older brother, had died of a brain haemorrhage. Looking at this dolphin picture I felt that so very soon Columb and Seamus would be dancingly free together, as the dolphins were.

Both boys were born with haemophilia, and this had given them much pain and stiffness in their knees, which they had hated. Ten years previously both brothers had been diagnosed HIV positive, after being given infected factor 8 blood by the hospital. Seamus had died suddenly without being told he was positive, while Columb had ten years in which to live with the threat of full blown Aids and the anguish that the fear of dying brings. Now, in the middle of January, he was ready to die. He used to pray out loud to his universal God:

'Oh Lord please take me.
　I have known your joy and peace in my heart.
　　I have known your presence.
　　　Please take me.
　　　　It's one breath away.
　　　　　Take away my grief and pain.
　　　　　　Help me to feel your bliss, love and joy.
　　　　　　It's only one breath away.
　　　　　　One breath away.'

During the last day he was capable of speech Columb told his mother and father over and over again how much he loved them; how he was sorry for things. His feelings were intense. It made me think of

74

the love a small child has for his mother before he goes to school, when she is his whole universe.

It seems that when you are on the threshold of two worlds, all the personality traits that have niggled during life melt away, and clear vision takes its place.

'Seamus is here with me Mum,' he kept saying, 'Seamus is here with me.' Then, 'Mum, there's a beautiful white lady waiting here for me.'

Columb's joy filled the room.

'Debbie,' he said, 'it is amazing.' She had previously said, while sharing a special night with him, that at the end it would be amazing.

'Help me to go,' he cried out.

Mary said, many times, 'Go with our blessing, with everybody's blessing.'

After this day and night of loving farewells he slept for four days, breathing evenly and strongly. As in birth, when we do not know the precise start of labour, we can have no idea when is the exact moment of departure. Columb took one breath and went. There was no warning, no signs of failure. It was as he had longed for it to be in his prayers:

'One breath.'

He looked beautiful with joy and peace on his face. He died surrounded by those who loved him, who had so faithfully shared his last days and nights. The room was lit by candles. His favourite music was playing, his bed decorated with mimosa and roses. I think we'd all like to go like that.

Much as Columb will be missed and grieved for, those who loved him could only be glad that his final parting was so tender. There are few people who have worked so hard at tying up all the loose ends with such results before journeying on.

His death has touched my life profoundly. He took us all to the threshold with him. Some of that joy and peace, which filled his hospital side room, was passed on to those who were near to him.

Mary said to me some months later,

'You gave him life to die.'

But it was Columb himself who achieved this by his courage.

Spring 1995.
In memory of his loving parents, Mary and Patrick

LOST AND FOUND

The phone call came out of the blue.

'I've got a little girl on file who might suit you. She's just five, the daughter of a traveller. She's been in care since summer and a care order has been obtained.'

'Can you describe her? I replied, hope rising in me.

'Well, she's lively and healthy, an only child and needing long term care, possibly leading to adoption. She's doing well at school and has a strong link with her mother who she sees regularly.'

She then filled me in with confidential information which had led to the care order taking place. My mind began forming mental images. What was she like? Was she small, fat, thin, dark, fair? Was she affectionate? Withdrawn? Sad-looking? I learned that there were as yet no photos, but that she was small for her age, fairish, with large brown eyes.

We were told that we would hear nothing more until after Christmas.

'Don't raise your hopes too much as she has to be offered to the county where she is living first.'

We all went out as a family for coffee to celebrate. I thought,

'Don't raise your hopes too much, that's impossible.'

I understood the meaning, but I needed to visualise our family of three growing to four. I wanted to get used to the idea, just as I would have done if I had found myself pregnant. The excitement receded as the weeks passed, and then in January we were hurtled into the next stage: The meeting with the child's social worker, the sad history revealed, and an actual photograph of her. A bright little animated face, slightly blurred. Then the first and telling meeting with the child was arranged. I was unprepared for the kaleidoscope of feelings that this visit brought up in me, now that the reality was staring me in the face:

PANIC.

How is our life going to be changed? How will it affect my son? Will it traumatise him? Will it be detrimental for him? Would it be better for him to stay an only child? Suddenly time alone with him seemed supremely important. Was this special relationship going to be spoilt? Would I still have time to do with him all the things I had imagined as he grew older. I had just returned from a 'writing weekend'. It was my first weekend away from my three year old son, and I was inspired by the freedom and joy of being creative again. Perhaps now I would have no time for my own projects. Part of me stood back and watched these feelings with understanding, recognizing them as natural.

We drove, full of trepidation, to the meeting. We were pretending to be going for tea with her short-term foster carer. The little girl was sitting on the sofa. I remember her red and black spotted sweatshirt and baggy dungarees hiding her shape. Her mouth was set in a thin hard line. Her hair was dull; a lifeless mass. She was silent with tension and I thought,

'Help, she looks so tough!'

My husband sat on the floor by her, and talked her into doing some sticky pictures with him. My son, affected by all the tension, clung tightly to me demanding my attention. I observed her from afar, watching her relax a little as she made pictures for us. I was still feeling tightly reserved and protective of my son. It was only on parting that the change came about.

As she stood on the doorstep, her small face puckered into a great sadness, she looked like a little waif. All the tightness and hardness dissolved around her mouth and she looked as though, inside, she was a small, sad and vulnerable child. She was revealing this to my husband, who she had warmed to through play. My heart melted. I wanted to sweep her up into my arms there and then and take her home. That was the moment I was committed to bringing her into our lives.

CALL MY BLUFF

How many parents have found themselves powerless before the might of a small six-year-old? It has certainly been my experience.

Impotent before the railings of my foster daughter I have felt helpless in knowing the way to handle her frustration and rage. In this particular incidence she had decided to pack her bags for the police to take her away to a new home, or as she said,

'I'm going to a children's home.' This closely followed a 'play therapy' session and she was reliving the many house moves she had previously had.

This particular mood had started at six thirty in the morning when she'd arrived in our room, all set to wake us, as she was in a mood for a row. It was a Saturday, so we'd resisted her barrage and she'd angrily stumbled out of the room to wake our three-year-old son. Then the dark morning had rung with screams as she fought with him.

Breakfast had been a nightmare. Perhaps stupidly, I had called her bluff and allowed her a bag to pack as she was so determined to show us she was going. Then I'd left the house to go shopping, taking my son and leaving my husband to baby-sit the little tornado crashing around on the landing.

When I arrived back I found she'd helped herself to more bin liners and the entire contents of her room was packed. She was victoriously sitting on the top of one of the bags, arms crossed like a defiant leprechaun.

This was the moment I felt impotence. Where did I go from here? Here was another Saturday in ruins. I felt frustration, rage and exhaustion. She announced,

'I don't want lunch.'

So the three of us ate ours, while she carried on with her sit-in on the bags. I decided to ring the emergency Saturday Social Work number for advice, and reached a calm deep voice in Bristol. It sounded more like the throaty voice of an actress than a social worker.

'I'm sure she wants to push you to the limits; so you can reassure her that you love her, and she is staying with you forever,' she said.

I saw 'forever' in my minds eye – a forever of tantrums, fury, defiance, spoilt days, wrecked bedrooms, and our exhaustion.

'I can't say that to her today,' I replied with feeling. 'I don't feel like that at all, at this minute.'

The lady tactfully agreed. 'It must be difficult,' she cooed. 'Try suggesting a little talk, and unpacking together.'

Feeling slightly mollified, I trudged upstairs. I looked at the mess wearily. Her triumph met me across the room. I blotted out her smile of satisfaction and said in a drained voice,

'How about trying again and I'll help you

unpack.'

Happily, she leaped off her perch, and tipped each bag out onto the floor. I look back and think that our great mistake was not photographing the chaos. There was not a bit of carpet to be seen under the avalanche of objects, collected from all her different placements. Games tumbled out of their boxes. Clothes, toys, books, empty drawers, bubble baths, hair bands, ballet shoes, legless dolls, bedding, pictures, all heaped the floor.

I asked my husband and son to go out for the afternoon, so they at least could feel it was Saturday, and I set to.

Samantha kept up a non-stop dialogue.

'Mummy, the windowsill is dusty, you'd better clean it. Mummy you haven't cleaned my shoes. Mummy this is too small. Mummy when are you going to buy me…?'

Drained with keeping calm, I went to fetch the radio, and plugged in the afternoon play. My salvation!

Three hours later, with summer clothes too small for our rapidly growing child removed, and the room sorted, she happily dusted her windowsill with a tissue and helped me hoover. The mess had spilled to all the upstairs rooms where she had flung any toys we had given her. Happily this had stopped at her doll's house.

I went to bed at eight that night. She fell asleep at seven immediately, spread out as if on the cross, arms flung wide, a contented smile on her face.

I looked at this tranquil face with wonderment. The stuck-out lip was gone. The eyebrows no longer lowered in a frown, and the frantic jigging about that went with her anger was still.

We told ourselves that tomorrow was another day. What will that be like?

THE OTHER WOMAN

When you are sharing your life with another woman, she is always there, hovering in the back of your mind. Sometimes, she looms large, as drama threatens your home life. But having never met her, it is possible to perceive her in any way that you want.

Over a six-month period, I have felt every emotion about this person. These feelings have fluctuated between anger, guilt, grudging sympathy, occasional compassion, and sometimes, after disclosures, white hot rage.

In the early days I had wanted to meet her. After a period of exchanging letters, I was not so certain. I was not sure that I would be able to hold my tongue without venting some of my feelings. In spite of this, I was curious to see what she looked like. After all, her life was bound up permanently with my family, and her name and life occupied a great deal of our conversation.

Then I met her - in the last place I would have expected it to happen. I had gone into the chemist shop for a nit comb, as head lice were back in my daughter's school class. It was pouring with rain, and my son and I were muffled in dripping plastic. He was dry, enveloped in his buggy, while water dripped from my rain-soaked hair and trickled down my face. I was unrecognisable.

There were two people waiting at the pharmacy counter. As I arrived, the young man left, clutching his medicine. This left a young girl. She was very agitated, hopping on and off her chair and twitching compulsively. She was physically unable to keep still. The pharmacist was keeping a firm eye on her as he made up her prescription.

She turned, and seeing my chattering son, smiled at him and then at me, his mother. It was the smile of recognition that one mother has for another. I stopped as if paralysed, then diverted my gaze hastily to look at the shampoos. I was totally confused. I knew that face. I saw the same features every day, in my five-year-old foster daughter.

An assistant hurried to serve me, guiding me to another counter. My voice squeaked as I asked for the comb and my hand shook. She saw I was agitated and said kindly,

'Don't worry dear, nits are very common. There is no stigma attached to them nowadays.'

'You don't understand,' I screamed inwardly. 'That's my foster daughter's mother over there! Don't you realise she's just smiled at us, and I've got her 'baby'!' I stayed silent.

We left the shop, and for the next twenty minutes I agonised about whether I should have spoken to her and told her who I was.

Although our child is under a full care order, I am amazed how guilt can rise up in me for no justifiable reason.

Perhaps that is one mother's acknowledgement of another. I feel that she must care about her child as I do about mine. I love her little girl as if she was my own.

From that moment in the chemist, I could see how wrong preconception could be. We cannot judge. If my life had been the same as this young girl's perhaps I would now be the one smiling at a mother and toddler, as I thought of my own child living with somebody else.

Not many weeks later I saw the same girl on a bridge, sitting on the ground, begging, with a scruffy cardboard sign saying:

'PLEASE GIVE MONEY TO FEED
MY TWO CHILDREN'

I knew she only had one child, and that child was living with me.

HIDDEN LOSS

The pink room lies empty now. It's just a spare room, useful for friends staying. The corner table now used for projects holds the typewriter. The ironing board stands up most of the time. It's a useful, practical room.

Recently a three-year old foster child stayed in the bedroom, while his mother was in hospital. Somehow that little head in the bed seemed a disloyalty to the one that used to lie there.

Shopping carries the same ache. Girls clothes – the things I would like to be buying but can't. There is no need. Then there are the Rainbows, Brownies, swimming, ballet and riding. As I give lifts to friends' children I think, this should be you in the back seat. You would have loved this activity, so many thoughts left unsaid, so many dreams and projects no longer valid. Like a snail I withdraw the thoughts, the memories, inside where they lie hidden, a gentle ache tight across my heart, an occasional sigh escaping to give release to a tight chest, while my face smiles and carries on the occupation of now as if you had never been.

The pantomime; the shows; the 'Pizza Express'; the seaside; music; dressing-up; home performances and charades. These all continue with our son, but without you, without your tantrums, giggles, bossiness, dominance there is a space, a reminder in everything, the loss of a dream.

Life of course is stress-free. No more visits to the hospital, the child psychiatrist, play therapist. No more endless visits from the social worker or the phone calls giving advice. No more disturbed behaviour after you saw your mother. No more trauma. But there is still a space where you should be. There is still one child where there were two; one voice, no one to argue with. No more stopping the car for car sickness. No more wails. The family belt has tightened from four to three, but there is still a space. Two years of loving, struggling, parenting, have gone as if they had never been. Only photos and memories remain as proof to show you were once here.

If you had died, people would allow us to grieve. If you had been our child instead of being the child of another, and in the care of social services, many would have mourned and acknowledged your absence, but because you were not, the gap closed like a hole in the ice. The moment you moved on to your next family. Your past traumas made the full time dream impossible, leaving only broken hopes.

Now you have another life, three families later, that has nothing to do with our life-style. Different clothes, shorn hair, after a year here of growing your Mohican haircut out into a bob. A different value system. Then there will be more homes. You came from a traveller's life and you are still travelling. You lived as our child and yet we cannot see you, so that you bond elsewhere. No contact, except news of you from your social worker, and sending presents for your birthday and Christmas. We are all meant to move on as if it had never been.

Perhaps this hidden loss takes longer with no avenue for expression. As I see your old classmates at school, with my face turned to the world as if we'd always been three, with only the ache in my heart to show that you have ever been part of us, I think of you. We loved you and we always will.

1997

Vietnamese Refugees

VIETNAM CAME TO ME

As an idealistic sixteen-year-old, I longed to go overseas and work in an orphanage. Doctor Apley, a paediatrician, was going to arrange for me to go to Vietnam, but then the war broke out there and it was never to be.

Many years later in 1980 I was teaching in Ipswich and a large group of Vietnamese boat people were sent to this town to live in a centre, which was a large old house on the outskirts. I worked in the evenings and weekends as a volunteer with these wonderful families, teaching them English. I mainly worked with two families. Each was housed in one room, where they slept in bunks and hammocks strung from wall to wall, with a string attached for the grandmothers and children to rock the babies. All the families cooked and ate together, pooling their rations and some evenings I ate with them. The food was very nutritious with lots of vegetables and a little chicken and fish. Sometimes rows would break out with the women screaming and pulling each other's hair. There was a lot of tension, as each and every one of them had suffered greatly. When I ate with them they teased me and laughed a great deal at my clumsiness when I tried to gnaw chicken bones holding them in chop sticks.

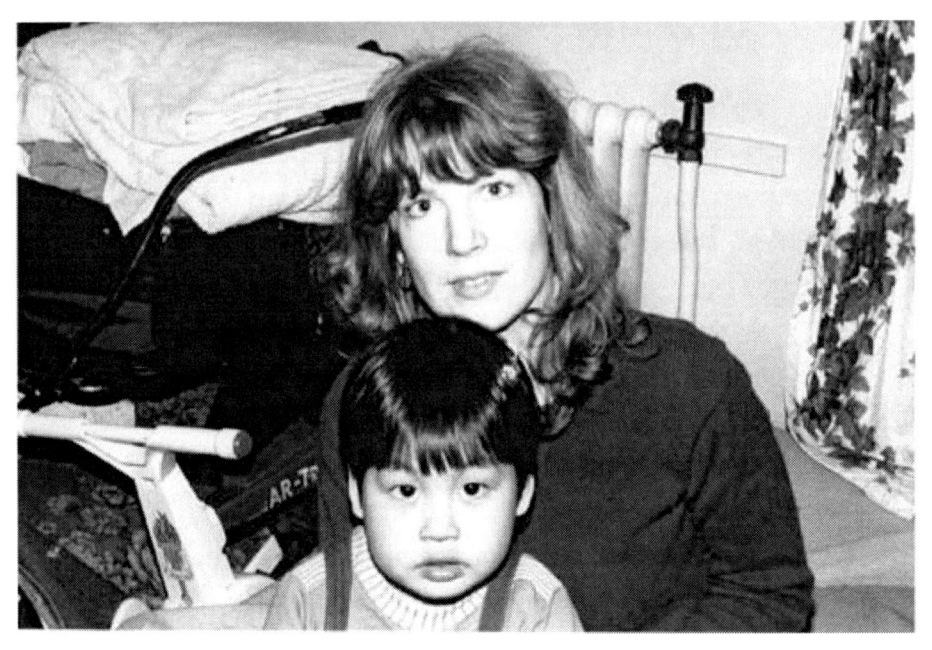

They would hand me the china spoons that they used to feed the babies and small children.

They loved to come back with me to my very basic student flat. They would open every cupboard to see what was in it and this led to a lot of vocabulary to help with the teaching of English. I also drove them around to see Suffolk. I adored these people. I spent hours in jumble sales and charity shops finding them really good quality, warm clothes especially for the children. I always washed and ironed them with care, and they would try them on with great excitement. Never have I done the ironing with such precision. My family particularly loved their four year old daughter dressed in a red tartan kilt and matching red jumper. She looked beautiful with her black hair.

One day I took a family to visit a friend who had recently been divorced. She was very sad and thin. She had three children aged from eight to twelve, and the Vietnamese were most concerned that she was alone without a husband to look after her and the children. Next time I arrived at the centre they beckoned me into their room and handed me a cardboard box filled with their food supplies. They had gathered this for my friend as they thought she needed feeding. I still think of this extraordinary gift from people who had lost everything.

Gradually these families were moved around the country to be placed in vacant council houses, often separated cruelly from their friends and relatives. I know they had a lot of opposition from people on the estates who set their dogs on them, breaking their windows and accusing them of taking their jobs, but the immigrant families I visited stayed stalwart, and gradually integrated as the children became fluent in English at school. Their houses were immaculate. They grew vegetables and the children did really well at school. Soon after this experience I moved to live in Holland but I can never forget the privilege of knowing these courageous families.

NOBODY GAVE ME FLOWERS BEFORE

'Nobody ever gave me flowers before.'

Shelly spoke with wonder and wistfulness in her voice, as a bunch of beautifully wrapped roses were placed in her hand by Midge.

Nor me,' said Kirsty and Jake together.

This was the moment when all the weeks of doing Tranquillity Zones for drug offenders seemed to make total sense. It reminded me again of how we take our loving backgrounds for granted. Yet so many of the young clients hooked into heroin had never been singled out as special and worthwhile in their whole lives. Now there was a bunch of flowers telling Shelly how special she was, and that she deserved them.

The Tranquillity Zones had started in a local town in England one year ago in January 2002. The idea was developed in Switford, and this particular group of heroin addicts from all over the county had started to attend Empowerment Sessions in Switford. After four sessions, transport problems made it impossible for them to continue, and without thinking I had offered to show them how to do a Tranquillity Zone in my local town in England, where the headquarters where based, as the courts were there. I had expected to do one or two sessions, but over a year later I am still doing them every Wednesday.

The first time I did it, I used the huts where they did daily sessions as part of the probation scheme. I had arrived clutching a CD player and vases and flowers. I was met in the car park by one of the clients.

'How much d'yer want for that?' He said, pointing to the CD player.

I smiled shakily as I had spent a sleepless night wondering how I was going to manage this on my own. Being part of a Switford Project was one thing, but doing one alone was quite different. My husband and a friend came to help me set up the first one. The room I had was smoky and unaired and filled with stains from coffee spills. It had food wrappings scattered around as well as piles of tables and chairs. It took a while to clear. All the clients who had attended the Switford Empowerment were keen to attend, and prime the new addicts about what it was all about. One lad stood guard at the door to stop anyone entering while we set it up. I brought in cushions and flowers and managed to transform the room with candles, colourful blooms and endless drapes. They settled, but I realized it had to be a space where they had no connections, so I could really make an experience where it was like another world. This is when the probation service agreed to give me another room in another building across town where these clients had never been.

After a couple of meetings they agreed to give me finance for a few materials and I set off to a local store and bought cushions, lanterns for the candles, a rug for the centre piece and four white vases. The room I was given had a soft blue carpet and white walls and blinds on the three windows. Although small, it was plain and ideal. A friend, Brett, agreed to help me and that's how it started. He became my wonderful co-worker.

Each week we arranged the room with a low round table with a white cloth and on it, away from twitching feet, candles floated in bowls of water and four lanterns also held candles. Four vases filled with flowers stood on the rug on the floor and the cushions were arranged around the edge. We used rose oil as a sensory aroma and each week I carefully chose the flowers for their scent and colour. Being spring we had daffodils, narcissus and tulips to begin. Then we chose different coloured wrapping paper, which would back up the separate art sessions, so that they could make their own choice of colour to take the flowers home in. I explained that the flowers were a gift to them. Part of the aim of the Bahai tranquillity zone was to accustom them to giving out, both to others and to themselves.

Each week they had music and a different story. Each story was about overcoming something, and designed to encourage personal growth. Then they had a fantasy journey where they went by boat to a beautiful island and met a wise person. Each week they heard the words:

'You are a mine rich in gems of inestimable value' several times.

Then Nelson Mandela's words:

'Who are you not to shine your light on the world?'

They also had the choice in their imagination of going under a waterfall of pure crystal water to be cleansed and they could drink,

'The pure water that gushed from the rock above,'

The whole journey was done in spiritual metaphors based on the Bahai writings and used indirectly so no religious connotations could disturb them. Each group of clients, a group of up to twenty, would have a total of four months on probation, if they didn't re-offend whilst on the programme, so some of them attended for sixteen weeks. There were often new clients coming in too.

When Brett and I first started the Baha'i Tranquillity zone, the whole experience lasted for half an hour. Whenever we gave out assessment forms the majority always wrote that they wanted it to be longer, so now the journey lasts for fifty minutes each week. Still the only criticism is that they would like it to be longer.

Over the months we have witnessed a huge change in those who attended. In the beginning they used to lurch unsteadily into the building, grumbling and fussing about waiting, munching on sandwiches and sweets, and hand-rolling up cigarettes with no eye contact or conversation. I used to offer them rose oil to put on their wrists.

'Do we sniff it or lick it?' I was asked more than once.

'What's it for?'

It had to be a substance to do something.

When I explained it was purely for smell and relaxation most of them would offer their wrists, and I would place it on a spot between bruises and tattoos and needle marks and show them how to rub it in.

'That's not enough,' they would say.

Brett would have the music playing as they approached and, fussing and bothering, they would stumble up the stairs and into a darkened candle-lit room. Then there would be a scramble as to who could grab the most cushions and get the best place. Inevitably one or two late comers would end up lying stiff and wary on the floor with no cushions. One or two would even place their coke cans and crisp packets on the candle-lit table. They were probably all thinking,

'What are those weird people going to do to us?'

'What do they want out of us?'

Suspicion showed in their rigid feet, stuck out towards the candle-lit centre piece. Although the room was warm they were dressed for protection. Coats on, hoods up, caps down to cover eyes and arms crossed tightly across their chests. They moaned, wriggled and complained. Everything was wrong. It was too hot, too cold, too crowded, too uncomfortable. I remember now how fast my heart used to beat.

'How am I ever going to settle this new lot down?'

I would offer up a silent prayer whilst trying to look calm and nonchalant, as if I'd been doing this all my life. I counted up to ten in my mind, and began:

'Close your eyes for just a while and let the

silence in' I said the whole verse twice. Most of their eyes were wide open staring unblinkingly at me.

'What is she doing to us, this mad woman?' they must have been thinking.

I'm sure when they had been put on probation for their drug offences, nothing had prepared them for this. Was this a punishment? One girl, Tracey, made a point of handing out sweets, each one nudging each other to hand them round. Others tried other distraction techniques, like arranging and rearranging their positions, sighing, or grinning at each other across the room. One or two got the giggles. No wonder I needed to pray. Then the school teacher in me rose to the occasion. They suddenly became a class of special-needs children that I had so often taught in the past, using disruption as a means of trying to cover up the fact that they didn't know how to do the work.

Brett turned the music higher, and my voice grew stronger and firmer as I explained that this was an experience to help them learn a relaxation technique. I put it to them that when things were too hot, too cold or too uncomfortable they were going to learn for a short time how to let go of resistance, and to breathe deeply, from their 'tummies', I used this word to show them where to breathe from, so they could use this skill in their everyday life. I had used the right words. They understood!

The first two or three weeks were not easy, but most of them enjoyed it, mystified as they were, and were back next week, queuing on the stairs, wrists held out for the oil. By the third week they were saying hello. They were beginning to think that perhaps I wasn't trying to get something out of them. Each week I would ask them what the word tranquillity meant to them, and remind them about letting go of resistance for a short time.

By now the sweet eating had stopped. They no longer placed coke cans on the table. They left them outside the room. Most of the coats were taken off, and used as pillows. Each week I worked on breathing as part of the journey. Arms were no longer tightly crossed. At first nearly all of them breathed shallowly. Most of them were heavy smokers. Some of them hyperventilated and felt dizzy. Gradually the breathing has deepened and now they all breathe from their stomachs slowly and deeply. A lot of them also play music at home, and practice what they have picked up about relaxation. Some have asked for tapes and CD's of the music. At each session a probation worker, counsellor or doctor used to accompany them. The doctor said that he felt this tranquillity zone was having a deep effect on them, as all the positive words were reaching them while they were relaxed. He was trained in hypnotherapy, so he was very supportive of the whole idea.

Now just over a year later, we are coming to the end of our third group. New clients arrive all the time. It is then that I am reminded of the changes in the ones who have been attending for several weeks. They now arrive eagerly downstairs on time. They wait calmly. They no longer complain. They look clean and well turned out. Cigarettes no longer appear. Food is placed downstairs. They say 'hello,' ask me how I am, give me eye-contact, smiles, and, if I wait too long, tell me to hurry up,

'We're missing time.'

Sometimes one or two have to see the doctor at that time, so, as they want to attend so much, I leave cushions by the door so they can slip in. They do so silently and are relaxed, with eyes shut in seconds. They ignore distractions, they never complain. Over the weeks they have ignored heat, fire-engines, police cars, a child having a tantrum outside the window and snorers. They share the cushions out evenly, and all but one or two have their eyes closed, and become deeply relaxed. Most of them have smiles on their faces. They breathe deeply, slowly and evenly, and they remain like that until the last piece of music is played, which they associate with the end of the experience. Then they remain quiet. One of them always hands out affirmation cards. We discuss the gems they have inside them. Each week I hand out ten. Each week I read out ten virtues to remind them that human virtues are gems. This came about from an earlier session when, afterwards, their probation worker asked them what they were good at. Not one of them could think of anything. One client said,

'All addicts hate themselves for being so bad.' Jack then said that all addicts were very determined. He explained that from the moment he opened his eyes in the morning he put all his energy into thinking what he could do to make the money to get his drugs. Nothing could or would divert him from this and so he would achieve his aim. He'd done this for fifteen years.

'Wow!' I thought. 'Think what he could achieve if he put all his determination into positive things. If it takes so much courage, determination and strength for drugs and crime, think what he could do in life if he was clean from drugs.'

I look at their strengths in a different way after this. Each week I read virtue names from a book called 'The Virtues Guide.' I explain how some gems within are really shining. and how some need polishing, but how they all have the potential to shine. I mention virtues like creativity, compassion, loyalty, kindness, peacefulness, caring, and I add in honesty and cleanliness. At the end of each week they have remembered all the ones except honesty and trustworthiness, which they shut out, but lately, to my delight, they have even said these. They have been happy to have been given ideas about their virtues. They have never thought about these before and now they are volunteering their strengths.

'I am a good dad,' said Mark. Kirsty, Jack and Jamie all describe themselves as creative. Others see themselves as kind, loyal, determined or courageous. All of them say they can be peaceful because of the tranquillity zone experience. Kirsty has started to write poetry again, and draw. Some weeks she brings her poems in for me to read. She shoves them into my hand without a word. I feel very touched and privileged to be trusted. They are lovely pieces of writing all about her longing to love and be loved. Her drawings are spiritual, swans on lakes in beautiful sunsets. They are excellent. Kirsty who shows the world a tough exterior is deeply compassionate. She mothers all the bewildered and vulnerable newcomers. One day, one of the new clients was very upset. He was on the verge of exploding and she stroked his forehead as he was next to her with such tenderness and gentleness that I felt a lump in my throat. When he suddenly stormed out of the room, she looked at me as if saying,

'Shall I go with him?'

I nodded and she gave me a beautiful smile as she crept out to follow him. All the others kept their eyes closed and carried on as if nothing had occurred. The first thing Jamie said the following week was,

'I'm really sorry about last week.'

I gave Kirsty a notebook and pencil for her birthday and she brings it in to show me her new poems. It's very touching. It makes me think of a story by Abdu'l-Baha when he talks about people being like chocolates. Whatever they look like outside, inside there is something very sweet, special and delicious. Every week I am reminded of this. Jack attends college for art and pottery classes. He has been drug-free for three months and is nearly free of Methadone. Jason is looking for woodwork classes. He loves building furniture. Kirsty is writing each week and is going to do a pottery class. They now talk about themselves as creative people. Midge arranges the flowers each week for people to take home. She used to work in a flower shop. If the paper is not perfect she insists on new paper. Beauty and excellence is now creeping into their vocabulary. She is now considering a course in floristry. Now as we stand on the stairs waiting to go up to the Tranquillity Zone some of them ask what flowers I have brought today. Some of them are learning the flower names and sometimes they stoop to smell them before settling down. Another session they have with the probation service is art and colour healing, so we try to link this session to it. The art therapist sees which colours they are attracted to and gets an idea about them from this. We notice they really like yellow, blue, purple and pink. Red is also popular. In the beginning of this project, none of them appeared to notice anything. They disliked orange. As new arrivals they seemed oblivious to anything but their problems, but as the weeks have passed by, this whole sensory experience appears to have awakened something in them. They notice the smell, the "karma of the room" as they call it, the colours of the flowers and different scents. Some of the young men are disappointed if the flowers have no smell. At first they all tried to grab the flowers at the end. Now they share and give each other turns. We have gently suggested that when someone is ill they might like to let them have some and for birthdays and special occasions. Now some of them give themselves flowers during the week for home. I never ask by what means. Kirsty recently told us how she got into a row in a pub with someone she owed money to. Instead of getting into a fight as she normally would, she explained to everyone in the room how she'd bought them flowers instead, and how it worked. I love to see these young men and women aged sixteen to forty going home proudly carrying their 'professionally' wrapped flowers. These were wrapped by Midge for their Mums and girlfriends. Kirsty used to take hers for her own room, which I felt was a wonderful first step for caring about her own needs. Some of the lads hide their bunches in their coats, so no one will see them carrying flowers. Image is still important.

One boy Simon used to take flowers home for his mum every week. He was a delightful person, always smiling and pleasant and a great advocate for the Tranquillity Zone. Every week we made affirmation cards with a quote from each story.

'I've got all mine on the fridge,' he told us. 'I try and say one a day, but usually end up saying them all.' Some of these quotes are:-

'I am potentially the light of the world.'
'I am created to shine.'
'I am a mine rich in gems of inestimable value.'
'I am a lamp and the light is in me.'
'How can I light the candle of my heart?'
'How can I make someone happy today?'
'I can, I will and I am going to.'
'What can I clear away in my life to let the light in?'
'Who can I make happy today?'

Each one relates to the theme of the story for that week. Each one has a different shiny sticker on. They are all done in handwritten calligraphy on coloured card. They are about four inches by four inches so they can easily go into a pocket. Kirsty has all of hers kept in a wallet.

One session she came up to me,

'Yeh, know that card on the mine of gems? I gave mine away last week, can I have another one?'

'I'll do you one now' I said, 'It's 'you're a mine rich in gems.'

I started to write it on the card.

'You've got it wrong,' she said, 'It's 'you are a mine rich in gems of inestimable value.'

I saw the face of one of the probation officers. His expression showed incredulous surprise. In the beginning he had suggested I changed the language. He thought the word 'inestimable' was far too complicated a word for them. I had replied that I wanted to keep it as it was: the only word that really describes the pricelessness of a human being adequately. It was from the Baha'i writings. After Kirsty had asked for these words, the probation worker never mentioned 'inestimable' again. From time to time I have asked everyone together what they thought 'I am a mine rich in gems of inestimable value' means, and they have all understood the meaning by their answers. I now know that most of them have all their cards at home. Some in their wardrobes, some by their bed and some, like Kirsty, on them. Even the doctor, probation officer, counsellor and social workers have kept them. They are sometimes able to link the weekly story theme with their group and individual counselling during the week.

One of the joys of coming in and coming out of the Tranquillity Zone each week is that I can experience these people without having to know anything about the crimes they have committed. I don't then have any chance to build up any prejudices or negative feelings that knowledge could engender. I could have the information confidentially if I wished, but I choose not to. I often think of Mother Teresa's words, when she described working with the homeless, as seeing Christ within each one of them. Perhaps this is what I want most for them to feel through these words, stories and metaphors. In a non-religious way, it is all about showing them how valuable they are, each one of them is innately precious. They have been created to shine. They are potentially the light of the world, and each one of them is filled with talents and capacities, some of which lie dormant and undiscovered as yet. Most of them started taking drugs and other substances as young as ten or twelve. Each one has a different story. I have no doubt that if life had given them self-worth at a young age, many of them would not be here. But I also believe that the human spirit, mind and body are always able to make changes.

Sometimes I feel so privileged to be with them. One of the probation workers once said to me,

'Go and enjoy these people, they trust you. You cannot imagine what trust it takes for them to lie exposed in front of you, their barriers down, their eyes closed.' I felt very humble when he said this. Sometimes, I look at them lying so relaxed in front of me, some in foetal positions, some hugging pillows, some cuddling up to a friend for support and some sucking thumbs. As with my children, all the energy and joys and sorrows of the day are replaced by sleep. It is as if I have fifteen to twenty children, innocent in repose. I feel great tenderness towards them. Almost all of them have smiles on their faces as the music and words wash over them. Sometimes when I read out the names of ten virtues they nod as they acknowledge that gem within themselves.

When new people join the group, I find that they begin to settle well after about the third session. At the moment Fred is quite disruptive. He reminds me of a child in school who had a pattern of being troublesome and getting laughs for it. He has tried very hard to spoil it for the others, and has made as much rustling and noise as he can for two weeks. Happily none of the others support it. They all firmly close their eyes and steadfastly ignore him. Without an ally he is slowly giving in. I can't help noticing he is the first to ask for flowers at the end, and he is put back firmly in his place by the others. Last week, his third, he closed his eyes and let go. The counsellor in the room nodded towards him and winked at me.

Perhaps it is here I should mention my own personal belief in prayer. I believe it has really assisted me on this project. Sometimes we have quite long pieces of music when I close my eyes, It is in these spaces that I can pray for healing. Some of them are ill from all the abuse their bodies have taken. Some of the girls are emaciated, and I wince to think how hard the floor is on their sores. Some have painful ulcers, Jim had toothache. Now he has had teeth filled and looks much better. One lad, Kevin, was deep in depression. I remember how last summer on hot days he used to come in with a thick sheepskin fleece and cap and hood. The first week, he opened up a magazine of heavy rock and gazed at it unseeingly the whole session, arms rigid. The next week he sat catatonically, arm hugged round himself, with a coat and fleece and hood. His eyes looked straight ahead unblinkingly. The next week he took his coat off, and the next his hood.

Little by little a layer of protection came off. He left soon after, but I never saw him close his eyes. He looked as if he was looking at some inner horror all the time. Another person, Sam, came in and made a point of leaving his affirmation card behind each week. He gave the appearance of arrogance. He seemed to be untouched by anyone or anything, and acted as if he was above everyone else. To my surprise, he booked himself into a private drugs rehabilitation unit and is doing well. Sometimes we have tears. One of them, who went into rehab., knelt forward and sobbed into the carpet. They feel safe enough to do this, and the others allow it to happen without reacting. They all know so much about physical and emotional pain.

Last week Brett was ill after a car accident. I was amazed how concerned they all were when they heard.I had arrived flustered and late from work that day, clutching my flowers and music tapes and the booklet with words. Everything went wrong. The room had been left stacked with furniture and the CD player for some reason was in the doctor's room where she was busy with clients. I was in the middle of trying to set up when my clients came in, wondering why I wasn't on the stairs as usual.

Immediately they saw my predicament they took over. One sorted the music out, the others cleared the room and distributed the cushions. One even volunteered to read the story. So I had a new DJ starting the music, and a willing team. Then, once they had sorted me out, they settled down immediately. At the end they suggested all the flowers should go to Brett and they signed a card I'd brought for him telling him how much they missed their DJ. It was a moving experience, and showed me the loyalty they had built up with the people who are part of the probation team. When Brett arrived back the following week they were really pleased and all concerned to know how he was.

'We've got to look after our DJ,' Kevin said.

This last year, being part of the probation team, has been a really creative experience for me. I have loved collecting the stories and adding the material given to me by the Switford Empowerment Project. I am personally convinced that it works, and, combined with all the other work and counselling done with these people has brought about real change. I think I could describe it as bringing peace and creative life back into their lives. Being told each week that they are of inestimable value, whilst deeply relaxed enough for the subconscious mind to receive these words, has to bring about some transformation. Certainly the sheets that the clients have filled in show that they all find it useful, and it has given them tools for the week ahead. They are better at relaxing and now know what peace can be. Two of them helped to make a video about it for fund raising purposes, so that more Tranquillity Zones can be carried out with groups of young people in the Switford area. Another video is to be made and several are keen to take part in it, and to give their views on the experience.

One or two of the Switford based people, who have finished now, voluntarily attend the public Tranquillity Zones in Switford. Others have said they would like them in their own towns. One of the probation workers and Brett have attended the empowerment training for youth in Switford, and were really pleased with the course. Last week the same worker described the Tranquillity Zone as a 'brilliant part' of the whole probation project. He said how it is looked forward to each week by the clients. They have named it their 'Chill Out Zone.' For me it has been a gift from the Baha'is, but also a gift for me. It has certainly brought transformation and change into my life. I am not for a moment under any illusions that a high percentage of these people will not in time reoffend more than once, but in spite of this I've seen such positive results over the eighty people that have experienced it, that I cannot help having faith that real seeds have been planted.

One year later I had a wonderful reward that made every minute worth doing. One of the lads came up to me in a shop and said,

'The Tranquillity Zone has changed my life. I

tell all my mates about it. I am clean, (drug free) and I am studying history and sociology at University.'

It is these moments that make life so rich. One story of many. I walked home on air, my heart full of thanks.

I dedicate this story to Brett, my brilliant co-worker, without whom I could not have carried out the project. Also to Tony, the probation officer, who made it happen, and to all the staff. And I want to thank Dr. Farzin Rahmani, who gave me support and encouragement.

In memory of Marcus

A BOSTON NOVEMBER

The wind bit through my trousers and padded coat deep into the bones as only the east wind can. The boat rose high on the grey troughs and then fell into the dip only to rise again at the next rolling wave. There were no white horses just the deep undulance. We were on the way to Cape Cod, something that I had dreamed of for many years. The boat was a research vessel for the Whale centre for New England and it carried about 50 passengers all hopeful of seeing these magnificent creatures.

A few miles out of Boston we came to a sandbank outside Cape Cod. Here many breeds of whales collected, drawn by the shoals of fish attracted by the sandbank. There was no shoreline only sea and the smell of salt and a few lone gulls circling on the wind. There were far fewer birds than I had expected.

Reinforced with hot chocolate, we made our way up precariously to the top deck, binoculars and cameras slung round our necks and clutching on to every handhold we could find as the boat rode the dark grey waves, before dropping down into the next hollow. Then the engine was cut and the boat positioned into an angle where it stopped rolling. We didn't have to wait at all.

The first hump backed whale breached just a few metres from us, a huge mass, so close you could see the barnacles attached to its bulk. A tremendous splash circled out from the water as it disappeared and the booming base sound that echoed filled our ears. We all scanned the dark water anxiously afraid of missing it. Again a few metres on it breached again and again and again, its huge body pushing out of the water, showing us its head and half the body before it crashed head first back into the water. The whale experts informed us that it was a rare sight to see this continuous breaching. No scientists have come up with the reason they breach. Perhaps because winter was here and the whales were about to return to warmer South American waters this was their farewell. The next breaching whale was a mother and her calf both leaping vertically out of the water in unison and then further out another male started his spectacular performance.

There are no words to describe the exultation that I felt witnessing these moments. The cold was forgotten. The watering eyes and the stinging wind whipping hair out of hats and making hands numb as they clutched the cameras were as nothing. I think all the whale watchers at this time were united in the magic of these moments. It is these experiences that mark our life in some way we can't understand, and lifts us to some higher feeling. Only the day before we had been hearing about Emerson, the philosopher, who had lived in Concord outside Boston at the end of the last century. His whole philosophy of transcendentalism was about the power of nature and how it can lift us to a different spiritual place and I couldn't help thinking that this was truly my transcendental moment.

I glanced at my son across the deck. I caught his eye even though he is at the age of being highly embarrassed to be seen communicating with a parent. I could see how moved he was. We stayed on the deck for two hours. We could see where the whales were by the spray or rather steam that rose out of the sea as these warm blooded mammals blow the warmed water out of their lungs. We could hear it like a snorting horse before we saw it.

The two whale experts had a name for every one. I remember the name 'Woah.' They never used a human name so there could be no character put upon these mysterious wild creatures. Every hump back whale has a different marking under their tail. It is their fingerprint. We were able to see these markings very close, as several whales performed their tail thrashing when they beat the water with their tails often for minutes, rolling over as they did it, so one minute you see a fin and the next the tail. Photography was difficult as you could never guess where they would appear next. They would silently disappear into the deep ocean as if they had never been. I knew my photos would be large expanses of grey sea with a little tail or fin or nose poking out, but it would be special to me. Happily on board there were marine biologists who were photographing our whales and I was able to order a copy.

Whales are in great danger. Many are dying from our wickedly polluted seas. Some found dead are so toxic with mercury and dangerous chemicals that they cannot be touched without the scientists wearing protective clothing. In spite of this they trust man as we witnessed. They had no fear of the boat. It is only we who can use our voices to speak out for saving these miraculous creatures and our oceans too.

The short time with the whales has ended, but the feeling and wonder is still tucked up warmly inside me. Nothing can take that away.

November 2008

Vietnamese families in Ipswich

Lightning Source UK Ltd.
Milton Keynes UK
UKOW050312220911

179058UK00001B/61/P